Candela's Secrets

And Other Havana Stories

An Anthology

Betty Viamontes

To Michael

Merry Christmas!

Betty

Candela's Secrets

And Other Havana Stories

Copyright © 2016 by Betty Viamontes

Published in the United States by Zapote Street Books, LLC, Tampa, Florida

This book is a work of fiction. Characters, names, places, events, incidents, and businesses are either a product of the author's imagination or used fictitiously. Any resemblance to actual locales or events, or to any persons, living or dead, is entirely coincidental.

ISBN-10: 0986423742

Zapote Street Books, LLC logo by Gloria Adriana Viamontes, cover painting by Felix Acosta, Cuban artist.

Printed in the United States of America

Written by the author of the novel, based on a true story, *Waiting on Zapote Street: Love and Loss in Castro's Cuba.*

"Betty Viamontes's narratives are like Noah's ark, a collection of all the 'specimens' to be preserved for posterity, constituting the profile of a people thrown to an uncertain fate," Margarita Polo, journalist, Cuban author.

Table of Contents

Candela's Secrets

When Adela walked down Havana's Zapote Street with her short skirts and wavy black hair bouncing over her shoulders, men stared and women rolled their eyes. Her flawless ivory skin and gleaming smile made the almond trees seem greener and awoke Havana's streets. Many neighbors called her *"Candela,"* like the fire burning in kerosene lamps on blackout nights. And true to this name, when the men looked fixedly at her, she would glow and turn her head slightly towards them, her long eyelashes blinking seductively above her sparkling black eyes, defined by a thin ebony line that stretched beyond their outer edges. Her perfume's flowery scent lingered when she passed by. Even her walk was provocative, with her straight, slim torso, bountiful bosom, and generous hips swaying from side to side.

Adela's husband, Roel, twenty-three years older than she, had contracted tuberculosis some years earlier. Frequent pneumonias had weakened his ability to fight his illness. In his early sixties, Roel's furrowed face and

1

tired walk made him appear much older, and retirement had not been particularly kind to him, as it accentuated more than ever the differences between him and his wife. She showed energy and optimism in every movement and loved to dance, while he looked gloomy, did not care about dancing, and any optimism he had enjoyed in his younger years had turned into bitterness.

He worked at home making guava marmalade with ingredients he purchased in the black market and sold it for two pesos a jar, anything to keep him occupied while his wife worked as a waitress.

Adela and her husband lived in a two-bedroom apartment on the first level of a three-story building nestled between two houses of colonial architecture. The houses had two tall, round columns on each side of their front tiled porches and one long window with shutters. Patches of different paint colors, mildew, and mold splotched the crumbling walls. The same disrepair affected the other houses in their neighborhood and the building where Roel and Adela lived. To get to their apartment, they had to walk through a long, dark corridor that smelled like cigarettes and mildew and had one functional light. Roel would take his time, as his breathing had become more laborious, especially on hot summer days when the temperature neared 32 degrees Celsius.

At first he had kept his illness a secret, even from his wife, as he suspected it would create more distance between them. He did not believe he posed a real threat to his family, since Adela and their daughters had been immunized, but the change in Adela over the past couple of years made him wonder if his secret had been uncovered. She arrived home late almost every night and would tell him she was with friends. She slept on their faded, floral-print sofa often and refused to show him any affection.

The couple's apartment had become a shrine to Candela's conquests: two pairs of blue jeans from the United States, an Italian red evening dress, a dozen bottles of perfume from Paris, and a refrigerator stocked with food, including two bottles of milk from the milkman, and beef and chicken from the butcher. All of this food had been obtained outside the allotted government ration. In Cuba, the government restricted the heavily-subsidized groceries to a monthly quota, a meager number of pounds of rice and sugar, a few ounces of meat, and small rations of other products, hardly enough to last a month. In the 1980s, virtually nothing could be purchased legally outside the quota. Sometimes, beef would disappear from the meat stores altogether, and people would be forced to purchase it in the illegal market at very high prices, or some, like Candela, would obtain it by providing sexual services to tourists. The Cuban people could only purchase goods using ration cards at scarcely-stocked stores, while tourists had access to *"diplotiendas,"* stores carrying canned meats, cheeses, and other goods that most Cubans had not seen since the triumph of the revolution in 1959. Candela would tell her family these were "gifts from friends and restaurant clients." But the neighbors knew she did *anything* to taste the fairytale life of the foreigners who visited her land; never mind her two daughters, one almost twenty and the other sixteen, or her husband, a recently retired police officer who at times seemed as ignorant of her secrets as her blind, seventy-year old mother.

Each time Candela passed by Havana's hotels that catered exclusively to tourists, she dreamed of the day a foreigner, enchanted by her siren body, long black hair, and intriguing black eyes, would marry her –forget her husband– and take her across the oceans to that prohibited paradise she called *los Estados Unidos*, or the United States, like the foreigners called it. People told Candela that the sun shone brighter beyond the ocean, and if she had the money she could go into *any* hotel and spend the night without attendants asking her, "Are you a tourist?" They also told her there were no ration cards limiting the food she could purchase at the *bodegas,* the meat markets, or the dairy stores.

Candela wanted to taste the joy of being on the other side.

But this seemed to be the only thing she could not get from her many lovers: a ticket out of her godforsaken island.

The revolution that her husband thought would help the country by eliminating private industry and passing the means of production to the government in less than twenty-five years had devastated the country. Unable to endure the country's privations any longer, many of Adela's friends had left in 1980 during the Mariel boatlift when over 125,000 people abandoned the island, even many of her lovers. Now, in 1983, the situation had worsened. Often, the food rations she and her family were entitled to purchase, like a few ounces of beef or chicken, were not available. Adela wanted more than a little rice with whatever she could find, or bread sprinkled with oil and salt. She wanted to wash her hair with shampoo, wear lipstick and eyeliner, dress in attractive clothes, and give herself the life to which only the tourists had access. Her husband, on the other hand, wished for peace and quiet, a loving family, and good health.

When Roel married Adela, he thought he understood the risks of marrying a much younger woman and had always feared their age difference would one day affect their marriage, but he'd hoped his full devotion to her and their daughters would deter her from seeking the company of younger men.

Her disdain for him as of late made him speculate that she had learned about his illness. The thought of Adela in the arms of another man horrified him, but in the end, his determination to learn the truth overcame his fears.

Around ten one evening, after Candela left her apartment wearing a white revealing dress, red lipstick, and perfume, he followed her. As she exited the building, he saw her turn right onto Zapote Street. The air smelled like wet asphalt from an earlier downpour, and its warmth and humidity felt heavy on his lungs. As he walked on the broken sidewalk, he noticed a handful of houses with their front-porch lights on and some neighbors gathered on a couple of the porches conversing and drinking coffee. From one of them, a large, skinny dog barked at him when he passed by, and he looked down and turned his head to avoid contact with the neighbors. But he did not realize that in Zapote Street little escaped the eyes of the people and that a woman who, through her window, saw him following his wife would soon spread the rumor throughout the neighborhood.

Roel told himself he needed to hurry if he wanted to catch up with Adela, and his eyes focused on her shapely silhouette ahead of him. She looked so beautiful, and the reality that he hardly resembled the man with whom she had fallen in love stirred in him a mixture of insecurity and pride.

Adela was still practically a child when he first noticed her, about a year after he became a widower. Roel's first wife had died during childbirth, along with their child, and those losses had sent him into despair. Work had become his only outlet, but Adela would change his life.

From the house of one of Adela's friends, located next to Roel's apartment building, she would watch him leave the complex dressed in his uniform. He looked younger than his age back then, from his chiseled face, tan complexion, fit body, and thick biceps to his muscular abdomen. She would always smile and wave at him when he passed by. He tried to ignore her at first, but she began to wear red lipstick and a white dress with a plunging neckline. She'd place her forearms on the front porch rails, her long hair cascading down in waves, as she bent forward. She enjoyed seeing how he would fight the instinct to look, the way his body kept moving forward but his eyes remained in a different place, a reaction that fell short of her expectations. She switched to dresses with a lower neckline, bending far over the railings and calling his name as he passed by. He could no longer ignore her and began to smile at her, shake his head, and keep walking. Her chest heaved with a sigh. Was he not taking her seriously? Didn't he find her attractive? Refusing to give up, she eventually devised a more ingenious plot.

The neighbors had gossiped on street corners about Adela's rebellious attitude. They knew precisely when it started. Almost two year earlier, after her sixteenth birthday, her father suddenly passed away from a fatal stroke, and she started to go out with older boys, getting home late at night, sometimes drunk. It did not take long for her to lose her virginity, which unleashed a new Adela, one not even her mother could recognize.

Lula, Adela's mother —who at that time was in her forties— had the external beauty of her daughter marked by the passage of time, with silver strands adorning her thick, black hair and thin lines near her ebony eyes. Complementing her fading beauty was the inner glow and kindness that had caused Adela's father to fall in love with her. Lula tried her best to fulfill the role of both parents after her husband's untimely passing, but Adela irrationally blamed her for his death and decided to do everything she could to upset her.

One morning, when Lula slept, Adela woke up early, tiptoed to the bathroom, and stuffed a small white towel in the toilet. She flushed it down and watched it disappear with the spiral movement of the water.

Moments later, water poured over the bowl and down to the tiled floor. She ran to her mother's bedroom and asked her not to use the bathroom; she would go out for help. She left her house laughing at her wickedness and rushed to Roel's apartment. Her desperate knocks on his door awoke him, and when he opened, wearing pajamas and half-asleep, she convinced him to go help her "poor blind mother."

When Adela told him of her mother's blindness, he realized he knew her, as only one blind woman lived in the neighborhood. He dressed quickly and accompanied her to her house. After greeting Lula, who came out of the kitchen drying her hands, her cane hanging from her arm and dark lenses covering her eyes, Roel went to work. While her mother brewed coffee in the kitchen, Adela followed Roel and sat on a dark wooden chair outside the bathroom.

She began twirling her hair, humming an indistinguishable tune interrupted by occasional deep breaths, crossing one leg over the other, tapping on the floor with her sandal, and raising her skirt slightly to show him her thighs. He continued to ignore her, and she sighed and crossed her arms in anger. Moments later, young Adela stood, turned around and dashed towards her room, slamming the door behind her.

Angered by his indifference, she set forth another plan. When the toilet "unexpectedly" became clogged again, she returned to his apartment wearing a short, checkered skirt and a revealing pink blouse. He came to the door eating a hard piece of bread sprinkled with vegetable oil and salt, his breakfast that morning. His eyebrows shrank in disbelief when she told him about the clogged toilet, but he dressed quickly and accompanied her to her house. Once inside the living room, Roel asked for her mother.

"She's out," Adela said stroking her hair with her long, red nails.

"I'll come back when she's here," he said with a serious expression and turned around.

Adela rushed to him and grabbed his arm. "I'm not kidding. You need to hurry! There is water everywhere, and I don't want my mother to fall," she said.

He shook his head, as if not convinced by her words, and started to advance towards the slightly ajar front door, but she scurried around him, closed it, and stood in front of it.

"Please stay," she said in a tone he had not heard from her before, not like a child, but like a woman.

He stopped and looked at her with a mortified expression. Realizing he could have easily moved her out of his way but chose not to, she took a couple of steps towards him, stopping inches from his face, so close she could hear him breathe. The smell of his faint musky cologne pleased her. She touched his shaven face with her soft and warm hands and looked up into his black eyes, noticing he was about two inches taller than her and more handsome than any of the boys she knew. His breathing tickled her and excited her. She brought her mouth to his, her full, pink lips slightly opened, and kissed him gently. Her eyes closed with delight, while a gratifying sensation invaded every part of her being, feelings that, she sensed, he shared.

He breathed deeply and removed her hand from his face.

"What are you trying to do?" he asked her. "Don't you see I'm a grown man and you're a child?"

Her eyes were fixed on his, as if searching for the truth beyond his words.

"But, I'm not a child. Today is my eighteenth birthday," she said calmly, looking at him suggestively, her index finger gliding over her lips.

She came closer to him until there was no space between them and brushed her lips against his. Then, she took his hand, which she noticed was bigger than hers, brought it to her thigh and led it upwards, beneath her checkered skirt.

"I like you," she whispered in his ear.

Right and wrong were fighting a fierce battle in his head. He liked her. God knows he liked her, but he did not believe what he was doing or what he was feeling was right, so he removed his hand, shook his head, and took two steps back, upset, confused, feeling a knot on his stomach.

"Don't you like me?" she said looking at him with an innocent yet suggestive gaze.

He did not respond, but watched as she seduced him, her hips swaying from side to side, the tip of her index finger inside her mouth. His breathing accelerated. And just when he thought he could no longer restrain himself, she began to unbutton her blouse, her fingers gliding over her skin.

His knees weakened. He felt overwhelmed with anger and pleasure simultaneously, as he tried to fight his desire. But then, she reached for his hands and brought them to her bosom, anxious for his touch. He caressed her breasts gently, her delicate flesh. He was now breathing faster, the softness and warmth of her skin fully arousing him, his muscles tightening. She was more beautiful than he had imagined, and her flawless fair skin drove him mad. Realizing that she was now closer than ever to achieving her objective, she unbuttoned her skirt and let it fall to the floor. She looked like a goddess to him and seeing her so vulnerable — her body screaming for his touch — unhinged him from his resolve. She embraced him and kissed his lips and he responded with desperation. And when she rubbed her undressed body against his, he thought the skies had opened. Oh dear God, what was he doing? He had lost his sense of time and place. His blood boiled in his veins. She laughed and watched his desperation for her, the masterful way his hands pleasured her, which made her feel as if he was touching her very soul.

His anxious lips sought hers and kissed them with an intensity she had never experienced, so different than the kisses from boys her age. She knew then, with all certainty, she was in love. The manner in which his moist lips brushed her body, starting with her neck and traveling down, and the sensation of his muscular body against hers made her feel like never before, like a queen, like an empress, happy at the realization he could no longer resist her, feeling the world rested at her feet.

After their first encounter, Adela began to visit his apartment often. She made him feel alive again, like the breeze of the sea caressing his face on a summer evening. But he was old enough to realize it was not love he felt, but something different; he lusted after her. Adela deserved something better than what he could offer; she deserved someone better and closer to her age. He struggled with the idea of walking away, but in a short period of time, she had started to occupy his thoughts each waking hour. He obsessed about the way she smelled, her smile, her fair skin and long dark hair. He wanted to be with her all the time. He could not think without her by his side. He kept telling himself that he was making a mistake and should walk away. She was too young to know what she really wanted, and her crush on him would pass. One day, after torturing himself for many nights, he decided to talk to her. He needed to tell her the truth.

He explained it calmly, like a teacher speaking to a student, not like a lover. As he spoke, he realized how condescending he must appear to her. Her eyes filled with tears, and she begged him not to leave her. "I love you," she said and began to cry with such emotion that it made him regret ever placing his eyes on her. It hurt him more than she knew to see her cry. Love, what did she know about love?

He could not leave her, either for egotistical reasons, or because he convinced himself that she truly needed him, so the encounters continued, each more blissful than the next. Finally, after a couple of months, he decided he did not want to live without her; he wanted, more than anything, to take care of her and protect her for the rest of his life. He knew the neighbors would judge him, but his mind was made up.

At last, he talked to her mother and asked for her daughter's hand in marriage. Lula recognized that her daughter was on the wrong path. Unable to provide her with the structure she needed, she thought an older man would help her fill the void and accepted his proposal.

The marriage seemed to diffuse the emptiness Adela's father had left, at least for a while. Lula regained her daughter, and eventually gained two granddaughters, that is, after her daughter lost her first pregnancy. Roel was good to Adela and her mother. He would do anything for them and for the girls, even purchase goods in the illegal market when the rations were not enough. Nothing was good enough for his Adela.

But time and the deteriorating economic situation in Cuba had a pervasive way of changing the dynamics of their relationship. Over the years, Roel's black hair and mustache turned ash, his face sank under his cheek bones, his eyes lost the glow of youth, and he seemed tired and absent, as tuberculosis and heart problems began to damage his lungs. Adela grew distant. He told himself that his health was no excuse for her to treat him like a stranger. He felt he deserved the same devotion he showed towards her.

And here they were now, he, an old man, following her through the streets of Havana shamefully; and she, a vibrant woman who desired something else out of life. After following Adela for a few minutes, Roel stopped in his tracks overcome by coughing and he covered his mouth to muffle the sound. He had not even walked half a block and already felt out of breath. Ahead, in the corner of Zapote and Serrano streets, he saw her turn left. He tried to walk faster, but his persistent cough impeded his progress. Finally, when he made it to the corner, he had to hold on to the trunk of a tamarind tree gasping for air. His shirt was soaked in sweat, his heart pounded and his vision blurred. He closed his eyes and tried to take deep breaths, but the cough wouldn't let him. He stayed very still for a moment, eyes closed, and waited for his breathing to return to normal. At last, he opened his eyes again and looked in the direction where he last had seen her. He squinted to find her white dress in the dark street, but he couldn't see it. It was as if she had been devoured by the night. Defeated and tired, he returned home.

When he arrived, he sat on the sofa of his small living room and waited. Patience would test Roel that night. He lit a cigarette, though it made him cough again, stood, sat, and changed positions dozens of times. The living room was mostly dark except for the light from his bedroom, slipping through the partially-opened door.

His youngest daughter slept in her bedroom. His oldest one, Alicia, was out with friends at a neighbor's party. He had told his oldest daughter on many occasions he didn't want her to go to those parties where kids drank rum and juice punch and danced, with the lights off, to prohibited American music. Anything could happen in those parties. Alicia didn't care. She seemed distant, making him question what he had done to deserve such treatment. He felt as if he were going to lose his mind, thinking about his life crumbling in front of his eyes, and imagining his wife in the arms of another man.

The longer he waited, the more impatient he became, asking himself repeatedly, *where the hell is she?* The last time his eyes focused on the clock, it was two. Now more than ever, he wanted to confront her, but his eyes kept closing involuntarily, and his strength was evaporating like a drop of water in the August sun.

At last, the door opened, and Candela entered, tiptoeing. When she finally adjusted her eyes to the darkness, she caught sight of his silhouette sitting perfectly still on the sofa. She froze.

"Roel, you scared me! What are you doing here?" Candela asked.

He detected nervousness in her voice. He took a deep breath and said in a calm, unemotional voice, "Where were you?"

As she reached for the light switch, he added, "Just leave it off. I have a headache." He paused and took a deep breath and said calmly, "Now tell me, where were you?"

She responded without looking at him.

"At my friend's house."

"What friend?" he asked. He could smell her sweat mixed with her perfume.

"Marta. Didn't I tell you before I left?"

He sensed evasiveness in her voice.

"No, you didn't," he said. "Why did you stay out so late?"

She shrugged, "I don't have to answer your questions," she said turning away from him, and throwing her purse on a chair.

He looked at her, perplexed. "What do you mean you don't have to answer my questions? I'm your husband."

She raised her forearm and waved her hand backward in dismissal.

"Just leave me alone, Roel. I'm really tired. You can sleep on the sofa tonight if you like. I'm going to bed."

Candela forced a yawn and walked away lifting her hair with her hands and pushing it to one side. Meanwhile, Roel, breathing heavily, his nostrils flaring, stood and followed her into their bedroom. She turned off the light, but he turned it back on, grabbed her by her arm and forced her to turn around.

"Tell me why you were out so late!"

She tried to twist loose, but he was stronger than her. He could smell alcohol on her breath.

"You're hurting me! Just leave me alone," she said.

Noticing some redness on her neck, his body tensed, and he grabbed her by her shoulders and shook her, muttering, "God damn it, either you tell me where you were, or so help me!"

"Leave me alone, you stupid, old man!" she yelled.

Her words hurt him more than she could ever know, and without thinking, he slapped her across the face. But then he raised his hands and stepped back in regret. Initially, he resented her for causing him to lose control, but moments later, he turned his anger against himself for allowing her to affect his actions. Adela sat on the bed and looked away from him trying to hide her tears.

Finally, overcome by her emotions, she buried her hands and face on the bed's pillow and wept, her back towards him and legs bent. Her dress was so short, he could see her white bikini, one he did not recognize.

"You hit me. You son of a bitch! Now, I will *never* tell you *anything*. You hear me? *Never!*"

Her words drowned in her tears.

Suddenly, behind Roel, Candela saw her youngest daughter.

"Mom, Dad, what's wrong? *Mami*, why are you crying?"

Rita stood by the bedroom door in her pink pajamas, her long, black curly hair partially covering her face.

Candela pulled the yellow bedspread up to her waist, while Roel closed his fists and clenched his jaw. He turned around and stormed out of the bedroom and the apartment, while mother and daughter embraced and sobbed.

* * *

As Roel sat quietly on the bus that would take him near *El Malecón*, Havana's waterfront, he remembered that as newlyweds, he and Adela had strolled by the seawall holding hands, dreaming of one day crossing the ocean together. Now, he was returning to this place alone, many years later, for a very different reason.

The day before, he had seen Yolanda, the barrio *santera* fortune teller, at her apartment on Zapote Street. He had heard the neighbors talk about how Yolanda communicated with the saints. Many people were afraid of her ability to look into the future. Some said she had predicted the death of a man once, and a week later, the man had dropped dead. Others said she had put a curse on him that caused him to die of liver failure. Regardless of what had really happened, she instilled fear in the collective memories of the neighborhood. But Roel felt he had no choice. He needed to know more about his wife.

He knocked on the dirty door of Yolanda's apartment, and the plump woman opened it and invited him in. His fear of learning the truth sent shivers down his body. When Yolanda closed the door, she immersed the room into darkness, except for four lit candles that illuminated the altars of the Virgin of Charity and St. Lazarus, and another candle on a square, wooden table near the corner of the room. Yolanda had chubby arms and a large belly that hung over her thin legs; a plump, oily face with small, black eyes; and bleached hair hidden under a white turban, except for wisps on one side of her face. She wore all white, no shoes and smelled like sweat.

At Yolanda's request, Roel sat at a round table across from her. The candlelight illuminated her bloated white face, her small eyes like two black holes.

She picked up a cigar that rested on a glass ashtray, took a long puff, and exhaled. Roel watched the cigar burning slowly, as its aroma wafted across the

18

room and made him cough. He looked at the saints again and at the three rotten bananas, an offering to them. The windows were closed and the room felt stuffy and warm.

The woman spread seashells from a small wooden container across the table, closed her eyes and extended her arms forward. She stayed like that for about a minute, then began to contort her body as in a trance. Roel noticed her short, dirty fingernails.

"Roel," she said in a calm voice. "You're very ill."

His eyes opened wide, and he felt like leaving the room. He was afraid.

She nodded repeatedly. "Yes . . . yes," she said as if she had seen something and paused. "You have been wronged by a woman. Pretty woman."

She frowned and nodded again, then moved forward and rested her chin between her thumb and index finger.

"Yes," she said; her voice was unemotional and her delivery slow. "There is a place near the sea. Truth awaits you there. You will never find peace until truth reveals itself to you."

Roel swallowed dry.

"Where?"

"I see a seawall. There is a huge building across from it. A hotel, I think," she said.

"*El Nacional?*" he asked.

She opened her eyes and looked at Roel with a frightened expression.

"Yes. You won't rest until you find the truth." She hesitated. "But no, you should not seek the truth."

Roel glanced at her with confusion. "Can you tell me what I will see there?"

"No. I can't do that. This is all I can tell you," she said.

Roel got up and pushed the chair away from him.

"This is bullshit!" he yelled, threw twenty pesos on the table, and left the apartment.

A couple of days later, as he sat on the bus with his eyes towards the city streets, he could not stop thinking about the fortune teller. What a waste of money and time, he thought.

The bus left him on the corner of L and 23rd Street, and from there, he began his journey towards the sea. He walked slowly, calmly, ignoring the tall buildings, restaurants, and hotels that stood on both sides of the street. He hoped that walking at this pace, he would not be overcome by the cough. People coming and going past him appeared bothered by his slowness, but he didn't hurry. He had plenty of time. When he was less than a block away, he could hear the waves crashing furiously against the rocks. The smell of salt filled him with anticipation, as an orange sun set in the distance just above the aqua-green sea.

Along the length of *El Malecón*, where shirtless children played on the rocks and lovers kissed by the seawall, he saw women dressed in colorful, revealing attire, signaling provocatively to passing cars. Other women offered themselves to the foreigners who crossed the ample avenue separating their hotels from the waterside.

Roel searched for Adela among the faces adorning the promenade. Now, as darkness set in, the yellow streetlights above *El Malecón* started to turn on. A red-headed woman on the sidewalk approached Roel from behind and tapped him on his shoulder. "Hey *papi*, come over here my love. I have a *papaya* that's better than Zoraida's," she said raising her skirt and touching her white panties seductively, her fingers with long, red polished nails sliding up and down between her legs.

Mortified, he pushed her away and continued his walk. She yelled obscenities at him as he walked away. Then he heard another voice directly in front of him, "Candela *mi amor*, you finally made it! I thought your husband would never let you out of his sight."

The female voice echoed through the promenade, and he looked up ahead, in the distance, and saw a tall, blond woman approaching. The blonde was speaking to a brunette who walked just a few feet ahead of Roel, and he curiously examined the brunette's body, the toned legs and the rounded, fleshy buttocks hidden behind a short, white skirt. When the two women were very close to each other, he stopped and faced the water to avoid being discovered.

"Sorry I'm late Marta," said the brunette.

He recognized the voice. *It's her. It's Adela!*

The women kissed each other on the cheeks, and Roel continued to listen from just a few feet away.

"How's Roel?" Marta asked. Roel tightened his jaw when he heard his name.

"Getting sicker and older," said Candela. "But enough about my husband. Who are we seeing tonight?"

Her eyes sparkled, while Roel felt his heart beating faster and his breathing becoming more arduous.

"The two Italians we saw last week are back for more. They're waiting at the Barraca," Marta said with a smile and raised her eyebrows flirtatiously. "Then after dinner, they are taking us to their rooms at Hotel Nacional. They paid the security guards to let us in through the back."

Marta had long hair like Candela, red, long nails, and wore a white skimpy outfit.

"Well, we should go," Candela said.

She grinned and grabbed Marta's arm, and then the two women crossed the multi-lane avenue. Some horns beeped and a couple of men yelled out of their cars when they crossed, "*Mami, que rica!*"

The women laughed and walked in the direction of the *Hotel Nacional*, a majestic, multi-story hotel opened in 1930 that, prior to the triumph of the revolution, had been a playground of mobsters, world leaders, and well-known personalities, such as Winston Churchill and Ernest Hemingway.

Gasping for air, Roel waited until his wife and her friend disappeared behind the magnificent cream color building. He leaned against the seawall, fatigued and breathless. He coughed a few times and placed his right hand on his chest. How could he be so blind? How could she betray him like this? What would their daughters think if they knew their mother was a *jinetera*? Maybe it was his fault; maybe he drove her away with his lack of virility. If only he had paid more attention to her, but no, no decent woman would ever deceive her family like that. No decent woman would ever let the hands of strangers explore her body in exchange for a few dollars. It was *her* fault. She had abandoned her principles and succumbed to the materialistic lives of the foreigners. These were his thoughts as he tried to reconcile what he had just witnessed. Roel looked at the vastness of the ocean and explored his options. He felt his body shutting down. It was as if he were in a tunnel surrounded by people who could see through him, to his weaknesses.

Wanting to flee from the *jineteras* and the couples strolling on the promenade, he began to walk towards the bus stop. The wise woman was right, but when she told him that truth awaited him there, she didn't tell him how incredibly painful it would be to face it. He needed time to think about how to handle this blow, but the tightness on his chest scrambled his thoughts.

On the way home, as Roel sat quietly on the bus watching the buildings move rapidly by him, fighting his anxiety, he thought about how to respond to her betrayal, considering various options and deciding on one. He knew how he would punish her for her infidelities. Why didn't it occur to him before? Now his muscles began to relax; his breathing returning to normal, although numbness, an overpowering numbness remained.

When Roel entered his apartment, he noticed a sheet of paper lying on the dining room table beneath the light fixture. He read it with his eyes, "Dad, I'm going to a party. I'll be home around 1:00 a.m. I love you." His youngest daughter, Rita, had signed it. He took a deep breath and said with nostalgia in his voice, "I'm so sorry Rita."

He sat on the sofa and waited. Through the long wait, he experienced anger, fear, and sadness. Adela's words still pounded in his ears, weakening him. How could she betray him like that?

Sometime after one o'clock, Rita arrived. Suspecting a fight, she asked him about her mother and Roel calmly replied, "She's out."

Rita bowed her head, shook her head, then raised her eyes and focused on her father.

"I'm sorry, dad," Rita said with a trembling voice and hugged her father.

In his daughter's heartfelt embrace, Roel realized what he should have known a long time ago. Rita knew! Everyone knew. How could he ever face his neighbors again? They probably laughed at him every time he walked by and talked about what a little, useless man he was. Roel kissed his girl goodnight, and she held on to him tightly and wept, as if she knew he had uncovered the truth. Watching her wipe her tears pained him.

At sixteen, Rita looked so much like her mother – the same long, curly black hair, the black, almond-shaped eyes, and the well-proportioned body.

"Goodnight, dad. I love you," Rita said.

"Goodnight my princess."

After his daughter went to her bedroom, Roel turned off the lights and let his body drop down on the sofa. He never imagined he could despise his wife as much he did now. He took out a cigarette, smoked it slowly, watching it burn, smoke dissipating in the darkness.

He must have fallen asleep because when he looked at the clock again, it was three. He went to the bedroom to check if Adela had come in, but the bed was still made, so he returned to his post.

Sometime later, the creaking sound of the front door's hinges awoke him. It was five. When Candela tiptoed in, he was the first one to speak. "You're finally home," he said.

"You scared me. What are you doing up?" she said and tried to walk towards the light switch.

"Come on *Candela*. Isn't that how they call you?" She froze. "Just leave the lights off. I have a headache."

She shrank her eyebrows.

"Candela? Why are you calling me that?"

He chuckled and shook his head before responding.

"Marta, your lovers, and probably everyone else outside this apartment calls you Candela. It really makes no difference. But tell me, why did you do it?"

"I don't know what you're talking about," she said averting his eyes at first. Then, she placed the palms of her hands up towards him:

"You know, I'm tired of your jealousy, your accusations, and your insults. I'm going to bed!"

She lifted her chin and scurried towards the bedroom while he followed her. When they were both inside, he shut the door.

"You think you get to walk away? Tell me how many men, Candela?" he said getting close to her face.

"Stop calling me that!"

The sound of her voice, the guilt arising from it, caused his heart to beat faster, and his anger became a monster within him. He grabbed her hair and pulled her towards him, placing his right hand under her dress.

"You're hurting me," she said on the verge of tears when she felt him burying his fingers inside her.

He chuckled with an irony uncommon in him.

"Come on," he said looking into her eyes. "Tell me. Is this what you want? How does it feel to be a filthy whore?"

He had pinned her against the wall, his body tensing when he thought about her betrayal.

"Was the Italian more of a man than I am? Was he?"

Roel clenched his teeth, his face very close to hers. He could smell a mixture of perfume, sweat, and alcohol on her. She swallowed dry and evaded his eyes.

"Stop hurting me!" she begged.

Roel let her go for a moment, then grabbed her by her shoulders and shook her. How could he be so blind? He imagined her in the arms of another man, laughing, giving her body and soul for the dress she was wearing, one he did not recognize, and he could not stand it. Everything began to fall into place now, her dress, her perfume. He reached for her dress and tore it apart with his hands, exposing her upper body.

"How could you do this to me and to your family? What kind of monster are you?" he yelled as she tried to cover herself.

"Is this what you want me to do? Is this how you want me to treat you?" he yelled. He squeezed her breasts angrily. "Is this how they touch you?"

"Let me go. You're hurting me!" Candela yelled.

He shrank his eyebrows and shook his head.

"I treated you like a queen all these years. You were always first. You were my life," he shouted, his eyes filling with tears, his voice cracking. He shook his head faster, as if the more he thought about what she had done, the less he could comprehend it. "You are going to tell me everything!" he commanded.

"What do you want from me?" she said. "How the hell do you expect me to live on your miserable retirement? You think you can support a family selling guava marmalade? Do you?"

Roel could feel the blood rushing to his face. He let go of her breasts but kept her pinned against the wall with his body. He closed his fists tightly burying his short nails into his skin.

"Tell me how many lovers? Was my doctor one of them? Did he tell you I was sick?" he paused briefly. She remained quiet, her defiant eyes avoiding his.

"You have destroyed everything. You and our daughters were all I had. What do you think this will do to them?" he said clenching his teeth. "Tell me how many lovers Adela?"

Without looking at him, she responded in a cold, calm manner, "You *don't* wanna know."

"Tell me damn it!" He slapped her.

The burning on her face fueled her anger.

"Fine, you want to know? I'll tell you!" she screamed looking into his eyes. "Yeah, the doctor told me you were sick. As for my lovers, there have been more men than you can *ever* imagine. Just face it. It's over between us!"

Breathing heavily, Roel clenched his jaw, and every muscle in his body tensed. He looked at his wife with hatred in his eyes and pain in his heart. He wondered what he ever saw in her and how he had failed to see the beast that lurked inside.

His eyes turned to a picture on the wall where a younger version of him, dressed in a police uniform, stood proudly behind the glass. Whatever happened to that man? How did he let her destroy him? He reached into the back of his pants. Then, slowly, he took a few steps back, gripped the gun with both hands and pointed it at her. Candela opened her eyes wide in horror when she saw the barrel of his weapon. She began to shake her head.

"Please don't do this! No, no, no, no! Please don't. You know I didn't mean what I said. Please, no!" She begged, placing the palms of her hands up.

He didn't move, just stared at her with the gun in his hands and focused on her almond-shaped, black eyes —his youngest daughter's eyes— full of tears.

"Think of our daughters," she said. "Don't you understand? I did it for them, for us. Don't you see the clothes they wear and the food we eat? How did you think we were able to afford these things? Please, don't do this," Candela said with a look of desperation. Tears rolled down her soft, fair face, the face he had adored for so many years.

"I beg you, don't do it," she said, as her voice drowned in her emotions.

He thought about his daughters, his illness, and his life. He could never kill her, no matter what she had done. It was him who no longer had a place in the world. He was tired of fighting, tired of the nightmare his life had become. Slowly, he began to move the gun away from her. There was only one way out.

Roel breathed faster now and could hear his heart pounding. He coughed, gasping for air. Adela slapped the gun out of his hands. This was her chance. She searched for the gun but could not see it. Adrenaline sped through her body. She reached for a dark hardwood bookend from his night stand, stood behind Roel, raised her arms up in the air and hit him on the head. Roel kept coughing while he held his chest with one hand, but she showed no pity.

"Is that how you thought you could solve your problems? By killing me? I don't want you in my life anymore! You hear me?" she yelled pronouncing each word with conviction. "I hate you! I hate you!"

Once again, Adela raised the bookend with her hands and delivered a second blow. He placed the palm of his hand up, signaling to stop.

"I hate you!" Adela yelled again trembling.

Roel kept coughing, his hand begging her to stop.

Behind them, the door opened slowly and Rita, their youngest daughter, entered the room and saw her mother standing behind her father with the bookend in her hands. She saw her father bleeding and turning purple as he gasped for air. From her angle, Rita noticed the gun which had fallen under the bed. It pained her to see her father like that, so frail, so helpless against her mother. She did not want her to hurt him anymore.

Shaking, she picked up the gun and her eyes filled with tears when memories flooded her mind like a roaring river. She had seen so much. She recalled when she and her older sister found their mother in the arms of a neighbor, while their father worked as a policeman. Rita was eleven years old then. "Don't tell your dad," she had told the girls. But it didn't happen once. The sisters had seen Adela in the arms of neighbors again and again. It embarrassed them to go out and see their mother's lovers who knew that they knew. Each time, Adela told them it would not happen again. Yet, it did. How could her mother treat her father like that? How could she treat her family like that? All he did was work to provide for the family. How could he not see what she was doing? When her sister, Alicia, was old enough to go out, when her father could no longer do anything about her rebelliousness, Alicia had found refuge in the loud music and the liquor of clandestine parties. Alicia and Rita pitied their father, his pathetic existence, but Alicia's pity had turned into anger and resentment.

Through her tears, Rita saw her mother raise the bookend up in the air to deliver another blow. She took a few steps back, pointed the gun, closed her eyes, and fired.

* * *

After the incident, rumors rose through Zapote Street like a flash flood. Days later, when the gossip had drowned in the daily routine, a neighbor saw a young woman wearing a white cotton dress with a flared skirt entering Colón Cemetery, just before the sun began to die. Her black curly hair fell softly upon her shoulders, and she carried a dozen white flowers with their stems wrapped in thin cellophane. She passed several tombs and marble statues that made their home at the Colón Cemetery, read the names on the graves, and stopped in front of one. The epitaph read "Roel Villanueva Gonzalez, good husband and father." She stood in front of his gravesite for a long while, caressed the letters of his name and wiped the dirt off the stone with a handkerchief.

"I'm sorry, dad," she said, her voice cracking. "She can't hurt you anymore."

A lonesome tear ran down her face as she deposited the flowers on top of the gravestone and walked away.

And some time later, the neighbors would see Candela walking the streets again, wearing a revealing red dress while her hips swayed from side to side. Her beautiful, curly hair cascaded over her shoulders, while men stared and women rolled their eyes.

Cousin Andrés

Angelica stood by a rectangular dark wood table cutting a piece of white linen fabric when she announced to her young daughter that later that day, she would take her to the children's hospital to meet her cousin. She warned her not to be afraid.

As a curious and inquisitive six-year-old, Laura wanted to know more.

"How old is he?" Laura asked, while she stood near her mother and watched her work. Angelica shoved her long, light brown hair behind her ears and adjusted the glasses that she wore only when she worked.

"He is nine, three years older than you. Now, please go play. I need to finish this dress," she said impatiently.

Andrés, Laura's cousin, had been admitted to a charitable hospital in Havana. During the short bus ride, after mother and daughter were lucky enough to find two empty seats, Laura's never-ending questions about

Andrés continued. It went something like this, back and forth like a ping pong match:

"Why is he at a hospital?" Laura asked.

"He had an accident"

"What happened?"

"I don't know."

"Where is he hurt?"

"I don't know."

"Is he nice?"

"Yes."

"Where is his mom?"

"Laura, can you be quiet for a while?"

The girl looked down and played nervously with her fingers for the remainder of their trip.

The bus did not leave them far from the hospital, and the sun was high in the sky when they arrived. They approached the entrance of the glowing cream-color building holding hands. A blonde nurse dressed in white led them to a large room with no windows that had an antiseptic smell and contained metal beds, lined uniformly on two sides. Laura hid behind her mother's light blue skirt the moment she saw the casts, burns, and young, sad faces lying on the thin mattresses. The nurse pointed to her cousin's bed, and the young girl approached him slowly, with a terrified expression. She opened her eyes wide when she noticed the bandages covering most of his body and the casts encapsulating three of his limbs. His bandages revealed his deep blue eyes and small chunks of red hair. Angelica introduced Laura to him. She smiled, waved at him, but he hardly acknowledged her and looked away. Her mother proceeded to explain the purpose of her visit. She told Andrés that after his release from the hospital, he would need to come live with them.

Andrés shook his head.

"I won't go with you," he said. "I want to go back to my farm home."

In a chilling tone that scared Laura more than the bandaged children, her mother said, "Son, you can't return home. Your mother has died, and your father, my brother, died a few months ago. You may not remember because of the accident. You don't have anyone who can take care of you. One of your mother's relatives has taken your sister and will raise her. I have offered to care for you. You'll live in our home with my daughters and your grandmother."

Andrés tried to hold his tears without success. Years later, when Laura would think of this day, she'd wonder why her mother had been so blunt. She would realize the tough nature of her mother, a poor woman accustomed to saying what was on her mind, without contemplations. Angelica thought it was better to remove the bandage fast.

Laura took a couple of careful steps towards her cousin, but her compassion for him won over her fear, and she carefully caressed his good arm with her cold fingers.

"Andrés, don't cry," she said trying to hold back her tears. "We'll have a good time. You'll be my brother. Come on, don't cry. I heard my Dad say that men don't cry. We'll have lots of fun. You'll see." As she finished saying this, Laura looked away and wiped a tear with her index finger.

Her mother glanced at them with sad eyes, as she contemplated the difficulties ahead. She hardly had enough food to feed her children. The war had not ended, and the post-war recovery that would lift her family out of extreme poverty had not started.

Angelica would sew day and night to put food on the table for her daughters and her mother. Her husband worked at his poorly-run hardware store that he owned, and half of the money he made went to support his three children from his first marriage.

After talking to Andrés for a few minutes and not getting much of a response from him, Angelica went to speak to a nurse, leaving the girl alone with her cousin. Moments later, she returned.

"We'll be back another day, Andrés," Angelica said. "Laura, say good-bye to your cousin. We have to go."

The girl said goodbye to the boy and kissed his good arm, while Angelica caressed his bandaged head. He then watched them leave with eyes full of tears.

They returned to the hospital three weeks later, when Andrés was released. Angelica had sewn him a pair of black pants and a white shirt to wear upon discharge. The owner of the farm house where Andrés's parents had lived for years had one of his employees empty it after they died, and had donated its contents to charity. No one in the family knew this until after a family member returned for the children's clothes and found an empty house. As Andrés reluctantly walked next to Laura on the way to the bus stop, she was able to take a better look at him. He was a "reddish boy," with reddish hair, reddish skin, freckles, and blue eyes. He towered over Laura and was much thinner than her.

When they were waiting for the bus, her mother told him, "Our home is very small, and the girls sleep on a mattress on the floor. I bought a small, used mattress for you. And remember, you will not be able to go outside by yourself, as you used to when you lived on the farm. We live in the city. It's dangerous to roam the streets. On Monday, I'll sign you up for school."

He kept silent. They entered the bus, and he took a window seat. When the bus started to move, his blue eyes seemed lost somewhere beyond the occasional palm trees, the people on the sidewalks —some walking their dogs— the elderly woman holding a white umbrella to protect herself from the sun, the beautiful colonial-style homes where the wealthy lived, so out of reach to Laura's family.

After the bus left the family at the stop closest to Angelica's home, Andrés noticed a group of shirtless boys playing with homemade balls. Angelica nervously placed her arms around her daughter and her nephew, and gave the boys an arrogant look. He shrugged, as he realized she would not let him play with them. The more Angelica, Laura, and Andrés walked, the poorer the area appeared. Finally, they arrived at a *solar*, a ghetto, where the poorest families lived in a series of dilapidated row rooms. Accustomed to his country house, Andrés's dissatisfaction immediately appeared in his eyes, in the unwillingness of his steps. They stopped in front of a dirty door, and after Angelica placed the key in the key hole, they entered her modest abode. It was located somewhere in the most impoverished sections of *El Cerro*, one of Havana's neighborhoods.

Laura's grandmother, a wrinkled seventy-year old woman with thin, white hair tied up in a ponytail, welcomed Andrés to their home. She hugged him, took him to the space used as a kitchen, only steps from the front door, and offered him a piece of bread that she had saved for him. That would be his lunch for that day. It saddened Laura to see Andrés's desperation when he ate the bread, and she wondered about her own parents. What would happen if they died? Who would care for her?

She whispered to him, "Don't worry. I'm going to give you a piece of chocolate I've hidden and a ball I found in the park."

"Laura is telling Andrés about a piece of chocolate!" Berta, Laura's sister, yelled when she suddenly appeared behind Andrés. She was only four, with thick, long black hair and a very thin body, so thin, she was practically all eyes and hair. Laura resented her sister, thinking that everyone at home used her constant illnesses as a pretext to give her all the attention.

Angelica grabbed Laura's arm and shook her.

"Where is the chocolate? Tell me!" She commanded.

Angelica could seldom afford to purchase chocolate, and when did, she had to hide it from Laura, as she could hardly resist the temptation. Angelica used it to flavor the family's milk on weekends, a deviation from the Monday through Friday *café con leche* routine. Laura did not respond. Andrés had not even been at the house for one full day, and Laura had already earned a spanking. In those times, punishment was immediate, without contemplation of any kind.

"Give me the chocolate, Laura!" her mother demanded, but her daughter gave her a blank stare and the spanking followed.

It was 1945. Scarcity reigned over her neighborhood. Although Laura did not realize it then, taking something that belonged to her family for herself was unforgivable.

Angelica did not allow Laura to play for two days, and unlike other times when she pleaded her case, she quietly accepted the punishment. Once it ended, she went back to trying to find out how Andrés had been injured. At first, when she would ask him, he'd shrug, and she'd let it go only to ask again a couple of days later.

She and her cousin played jacks one day when she asked him again.

"I fell from an almond tree and broke some bones," he said. "I hit my head too, and the doctors said that made me forget some things."

"Why were you on the tree?" Laura asked.

"I don't remember," he said. "I just was."

It would not be until several days later that she would learn about the circumstances surrounding his accident. Late at night, when her mother thought everyone slept, she told the story to Laura's father. The boy's father had died of a strange illness that attacked his brain, and his mother, from an infection, only a few months later. When a relative came to tell him of her death, Andrés was crushing with rocks under a tree.

The boy yelled, "You're lying!"

He ran as fast as he could towards the river. His sister, who was two years older, dashed after him and begged him to stop, but he didn't listen. When he arrived near the river's edge, he climbed the tallest tree and the twigs scratched his body. He finally reached the top and tightly held on to the branches, but his tears clouded his vision. Moments later, when he tried to wipe his eyes, he lost his grip, falling to the ground. A relative had rushed him to the hospital.

Since that night, Laura's determination to make her cousin feel welcome grew, but the boy's addition to the family seemed to bring out the worst in her, straining the relationship between the girl and her mother. One night, during dinner, thinking no one could see her, she took a piece of her bread and hid it under her clothes, with the intention of giving it to Andrés later.

"What are you hiding?" Angelica yelled, and Laura simply looked at her and shook her head in denial.

"Eat your food!" Her mother yelled, but Laura thought that Andrés needed it more, as he was taller. She shook her head again, reluctant to comply with her mother's instructions, and another spanking followed.

Andrés and Angelica argued frequently.

"Wash the dishes," or "do your homework," Angelica commanded. "No!" he replied each time.

She had done everything possible to show him that she was willing to trust him, but every time she gave him a task that required a certain level of responsibility, he would disappoint her. On one occasion, she asked him to take Laura and her sister to the movies. Half way through it, Andrés got bored and left. After the movie ended, employees could not locate someone responsible for the girls and contacted the police. Two policemen took the girls home.

Andrés also came and went as he pleased, making Angelica wish she had never offered to raise him.

For Laura's seventh birthday, Andrés brought home a small, fluffy dog with white pointy ears that he had found on the street. He and Laura named it Bobby. After they bathed him three times in their kitchen sink and dried his hair with an old rag, he ran around sniffing every corner and becoming acquainted with his new surroundings. When his hair dried, he looked like the dogs wealthy women carried when they strolled in the park.

When Angelica first saw the dog, she placed her arms over her head to convey her disapproval. How could she afford to keep him when her family hardly had enough to eat? But feeling bad for the little animal, she shared leftovers with him and tried to avoid becoming too attached. The way Bobby licked her hands when she fed him, the manner his little body made circles around her when she returned from a client's house, the loving looks his brown eyes gave her when she stayed up late sewing, these moments, and many other gestures of reaffirmed devotion, created an indestructible bond between Angelica and Bobby.

Cousin Andrés

Andrés bathed Bobby at first, but once the novelty of the new pet wore off, he no longer cared for him, no matter how many times Angelica asked him to bathe him or feed him. She could have assigned some of the work to Laura, but Angelica thought that her daughter was too young and assumed all of Bobby's care herself.

Angelica would smile when Bobby jumped on her wagging his tail, or when he licked her face, thankful for her care, or the many times he fell asleep on her feet. These bonding moments seemed to provide her with a way to escape her daily preoccupations. Bobby was always there for her, on the nights her husband did not come home after work, and she laid on her mattress alone staring at the ceiling, or when the girls went to school and she sat in front of her sewing machine, and Bobby, as if he realized the importance of her work, lay quietly near her feet.

Angelica had attempted to make Andrés's transition into her family as smooth as possible by using different approaches, from kindness to toughness, but nothing seemed to work. He kept his distance and remained in his own dimension, uninterested in family life and often lost in thought. Through threats, Angelica would compel him to complete his homework, but he did it reluctantly, purposely writing wrong answers at times.

He had kept the homemade ball Laura had given to him and played with it by himself often, bouncing it from one hand to the other, or throwing it up into the air and catching it with the same hand, while he remained expressionless, as if nothing in the world could give him pleasure. Only Laura seemed to get through to him, with her endless questions and displays of affection, but his answers to her inquiries were short and monotonous.

The passage of time did nothing to sooth his despair; if anything, it made him more determined to do as he pleased and to remain disconnected from his new family and from Bobby, who after trying everything he could to get his attention, must have come to the realization that Andrés would never pet him or play with him again.

Two years after Andrés and Bobby entered into their lives, Andrés remained as unmanageable as the first day. That morning, Angelica had asked Andrés to play with Laura, while she finished cooking. Laura's father was at the hospital with Berta who needed some blood work. Bored from being inside, Andrés missed playing with other boys. To avoid alerting Angelica, who was chopping onions at the time, Andrés snuck out of the apartment without fully closing the door. Bobby followed him, and Laura ran after Bobby.

When Angelica noticed the open door and Andrés, Bobby and Laura missing, she rushed out.

Bobby ran through the streets followed by eight-year-old Laura who called his name time and time again. He would stop briefly, look at her and take off running. The routine continued for a while, and now he had left Laura's neighborhood behind and had run towards the railroad tracks. Laura heard the noise of the approaching steam engine train, the sound of metal against metal and the whistling, but she kept dashing after him. Bobby's furry ears flapped up and down as he ran. The train was getting closer, and the sound of the engine grew louder.

Cousin Andrés

Laura's dark brown ponytail swung from side to side, and her pink blouse stuck to her sweaty back as she ran. Poor Laura, she did not see the approaching train. Her eyes focused on Bobby, on his white, furry body and fluffy ears. He stood diagonally to her right, across the tracks, his tongue sticking out as he breathed heavily waiting for her next move, as if asking, "well, are you coming?" The tracks were now only a few feet away. The engine grew louder. Everything happened fast, the sound of the screeching breaks, the screams of people who saw her.

Laura could see the train now, but she was certain she could make it to the other side to rescue Bobby. If only she ran faster. She was breathless, sweat rolling down the side of her red cheeks. Yes, she would make a run for it! Then, at the very last minute, she realized the train was too close and suddenly stopped, right in front of it. Her little heart was pounding. She could feel the wind that the passing train created against her chunky, reddened cheeks. The dust the train lifted made her cough, as she tried to search for Bobby in between each wagon, but she could not see him. She yelled his name and did not hear him bark. The wagons kept moving by her, one after the other, as her anxious eyes searched for Bobby.

Angelica, who had been desperately searching for Laura, asking everyone she saw along the way if they had seen her, found her at the precise moment when her daughter ran towards the tracks. She saw the approaching train and screamed her name. Then trembling and realizing she was too far away to help her,

43

she closed her eyes and covered her face with her hands, anticipating the worst. Moments later, after the train had passed, Angelica opened her eyes and frantically searched for her daughter. She could not see her, as by then she had already crossed to the other side to look for Bobby.

Angelica was horrified and yelled her daughter's name again and again. Neighbors gathered around her trying to calm her down, as she placed her hand on her chest, emotions rolling down her face. They tried to reassure her that she was fine. She refused to listen, her eyes focused near the tracks, where she had last seen her daughter. When after a while she could not see her, she fell to her knees and began to weep.

Meanwhile, on the other side of the tracks, far from her mother's sight, Laura searched for Bobby, and when she could not find him, she returned to the tracks, her head down. It was then she looked at the railroad tracks, only a few steps from where she had crossed, and realized what had occurred. She also saw her mother in the distance being consoled by neighbors, her knees on the ground and her face between her hands. Laura crossed the tracks and began to walk towards her mother. The neighbors saw her coming and one touched Angelica's shoulder. She lifted her head, and when she caught a glimpse of her daughter, she got up and ran to her. She embraced her, not noticing how much Laura was trembling.

"I'm so glad you are safe!" Angelica said. "You scared me so much!" She paused to look at her daughter and examine her face, arms and legs and when she confirmed she had not been injured, she asked her, "Where's Bobby?"

Laura remained silent for a moment, and then she broke into tears.

"He's dead," said Laura, her voice cracking.

"But no, no! It can be!"

She began to cry as if she had lost a child, and Laura cried with her.

Later that evening, when Laura's father came home, everyone was quiet, Angelica busy with her sewing, Laura's grandmother ironing clothes, and Berta, Andrés and Laura playing with a home-made ball. Angelica approached her husband, kissed him on the cheek and whispered something to him. He lifted his eyes and looked in Andrés's direction with an angry look, his nostrils flaring.

When Laura saw her father take off his belt and raise his hand, she ran in front of her cousin to defend him, but her father lifted her out of his way and proceeded. Laura looked down as she heard her cousin's plea for forgiveness and heard the belt slapping him. She could imagine his deep blue eyes full of tears, his reddish face turning even redder.

After his punishment, Andrés sat quietly by a corner facing the wall. Laura sat by his side watching him wipe his tears. He tried to be tough, but an overwhelming sadness filled him.

The next day when Laura woke up, Andrés was gone. He had left suddenly, the same way he had come into her life, and years would pass before she would see him again.

Pizza Coupons

As was her ritual before breakfast, Silvia Hernandez turned her Motorola radio on. It took a few seconds for the old vacuum tubes to tune in to the intended frequency, but after a loud squawk, the commentator's voice chimed in. "You're listening to Radio Rebelde, from Havana, Cuba, a free territory in America." She reached behind her thirty-five-year-old refrigerator and removed a six-inch piece of old bread from atop its rear grille. She usually placed leftover bread there to keep it toasted; otherwise, it would turn too hard to eat. As she set the bread on the kitchen counter, she continued to listen.

"The revolution, to reward the citizens and demonstrate its strength to the North American imperialism, has distributed coupons to the Committees of Defense of the Revolution, or CDRs, on each block. The coupons, which provide the bearer the right to purchase a small personal pizza at local pizzerias, will be distributed by CDRs to comrades who do volunteer work and support the revolutionary cause."

Pizza Coupons

Silvia looked at her coupon on the kitchen counter, and she imagined a freshly baked pizza. She could smell the melting cheese and delicious sauce. Soon, she would have a chance to eat it.

Following the fall of communism in the Soviet Union, Cuba was adrift, like an orphan child wandering the streets alone. Now the Periodo Especial, the name the government had given the difficult period following this collapse, was showing its vibrant colors: empty shelves at the bodegas, shortages of all basic goods, growing discontent.

Silvia washed a coffee cup, placed it upside down on the sink, and reached for the oil and salt jars, as the commentator for the government-controlled radio station talked about the rough times ahead. The Cuban government encouraged its people to remain patient and dedicated to the cause of socialism.

A noise interrupted the commentator's voice. Silvia walked over to the radio and tried to tune it, unsuccessfully.

"Static," she said, and turned it off.

She poured some oil and sprinkled salt on the bread, served herself a glass of water, and sat on a green rocking chair beside her dirt-encrusted second-story balcony to eat her breakfast. It was seven. The streets were almost deserted, except for an occasional passing car and an old woman who walked her underfed dog on the broken sidewalk, past the unpainted and dilapidated colonial houses of Zapote Street.

After eating the bread, she read a book that had belonged to her husband. *Territorial Expansion of the*

United States was not a subject she particularly enjoyed, but she missed him, and reading his books, touching the yellow pages he used to touch, made her feel closer to him.

Around eleven o'clock, Silvia left her apartment wearing a white sleeveless blouse and lavender cotton pants, both a product of her sewing. A single yellow light illuminated the long corridor in front of her. She adjusted her glasses, walked a few steps, and knocked on a dirty door two apartments down from hers. Silvia's friend, Marta, opened wearing curlers on her head. She welcomed Silvia with "Buenos días" and a kiss on her cheek. "Come in," she said, swinging the door open. "Do you want some coffee?"

"No, thanks," said Silvia, following Marta into the apartment.

Marta was somewhat overweight, age sixty-four, the same as Silvia, but fifty pounds heavier, and with less-pronounced wrinkles.

"I should hurry," said Marta.

"Yes, you should. You know how the lines get, and for pizza, who knows? Are you almost done?" said Silvia.

"I'll be done in a minute. Make yourself at home; I'll be right back."

Silvia walked a few steps across the small living room and sat on a faded blue sofa. As Marta rushed towards the back of the house she yelled, "Hurry up, José. Silvia is here!"

Silvia looked around the room, bored. The apartment smelled like freshly brewed coffee. She could

see most of the space from where she sat. The small
dining room contained a square wooden table and four
metal chairs with torn vinyl covers. The discolored walls,
blue with peeled, green sections, had a dozen black-and-
white pictures, all of them of Marta and her family,
except for two. Silvia focused on the first one. She had
seen it many times before, and each time she wondered
why Marta still kept it. It was Fidel Castro, thirty years
earlier, with a full head of black hair and an intriguing
black beard. It was hung right next to a picture of Jesus
Christ. Silvia shook her head. Her reaction to seeing these
pictures in such close proximity had changed over time,
especially in the last year. *There they are again, the devil and
Jesus Christ*, she thought. But Silvia didn't want to judge.
Marta was a good friend, regardless of her political
ideology. Unlike Silvia, she believed in the revolution
and volunteered in the neighborhood watches, which
were designed to curtail antirevolutionary activity. Silvia
mistrusted the government and its message, and she
volunteered only in order to survive within the system.
She did not want to be a white hat on a shelf full of red
ones, even if some of the red ones were actually white
underneath.

Silvia heard some noise in the back of the
apartment and, almost immediately, Marta and her
husband, José, appeared, Marta holding a brown purse
under her arm and José combing his full head of white
hair.

"Always in a hurry," he complained, setting his
comb on the dining-room table.

Pizza Coupons

"We must get there early. The earlier we do, the sooner we'll get the pizza," said Marta.

Silvia rose from her seat. "Good morning, José."

He walked towards Silvia and kissed her on the cheek. "Good morning, señorita. You look splendid today," he said with a wide smile.

Silvia placed her hands on her hips and said, "I don't feel like joking around today. I'm too old for that."

Marta laughed, lifted the comb off the table and placed it in her purse. After years of telling her husband to keep the house orderly, but failing to get his attention, she had grown accustomed to picking up after him. José shook his head and scratched his white mustache.

"Silvia, Silvia. What is old but a state of mind?" he said.

"Stop philosophizing and open the door, my little old man," said Marta, as she tapped her husband on his shoulder. "Come on. It's time to go."

He shook his head and rolled his eyes. "Women," he said.

After exiting the apartment, they walked down the narrow hallway that led to the stairs.

"I can already smell that pizza. You know how long it's been since the last time I had some? Over a year!"

"Me too," said Silvia.

"What do you want ladies? It's the cheese!" said José, raising his index finger into the air. "Remember the time, Marta, when Cuba was still buying subsidized cheese from Bulgaria and Russia, and we ate pizza every couple of months? Those were the days!"

Pizza Coupons

"And without a coupon," added Marta.

When they arrived to the end of the hallway, they began to descend the stairs slowly, Marta going first, followed by José and then Silvia. Halfway down, José yawned, stretched his arms, and said, "Yes, those were the times. But I'm sure this is just a temporary situation. Things can't stay the way they are for too long." His voice echoed between the walls of the stairwell.

Silvia rolled her eyes and said, "Yes indeed, very temporary. What do you think of that, Marta?"

As she approached the bottom of the stairs, Marta looked back to reply. Her foot missed the step and she began to tumble down, as if in slow motion. José could not react quickly enough as her body skipped a couple of steps and fell sideways on the flat area beneath the stairs.

"Oh no!" yelled Silvia with a hand on her chest. "Ay José chico, hurry!"

Marta's face tensed from the pain. She rubbed her knee while tears ran down her cheeks.

"My knee. It hurts a lot. I think it's broken," she said.

José knelt on the dull granite floor beside his wife and caressed her shoulder.

"Mi amor, I'm sorry," he said.

Silvia stood near them, her hands framing her face.

"Let me think," she said, scratching her head. After a few seconds, her eyes lit up. "I know. I'll go back to my apartment and get some duralgina for the pain and a pair of crutches. José, you need to take her to the hospital right away!"

51

"Great. Now I won't be able to eat pizza," complained Marta, wiping her tears from her chubby cheeks.

"Don't worry. I'll hold a spot for you," said Silvia.

"Both of you, stop talking about the damn pizza! If we don't get to eat it, so be it. Maybe if you had not made such a fuss about it . . ." He shook his head and scratched his mustache. "Just forget it. Silvia, please get the crutches."

Silvia gave him a reproachful look before walking away. Moments later, when she returned, José was patting his wife's back.

"It hurts," Marta said holding on to the wall.

José kissed her forehead and helped get more comfortable.

"Mi amorcito, I don't like to see you in pain. I'm so sorry."

Marta curled her lip and rubbed her fleshy knee.

"Ay José. I really want some pizza. Can you let Silvia hold a spot for us? Please?"

José thought about it for a moment. Since the fall of the Soviet Union, he and Marta had often had little but an old piece of bread sprinkled with salt and oil for dinner. He finally conceded, which cause his wife to smile despite the pain. Moments later, Silvia returned with wooden crutches under her arm, along with a cup of water and a pill for the pain.

José and Marta said good-bye to their friend and took a public bus to the William Soler Hospital, while Silvia walked in the direction of the Sorrento Pizzeria, located near Calzada de Diez de Octubre. In her black vinyl purse, she had the coupon that entitled her to purchase a small pizza for one-and-a-quarter pesos. On the corner of Zapote and Serrano streets she saw two kids crushing almonds with rocks under the shade of an almond tree and thought about her sons.

On her way to the pizzeria, she passed many colonial-style houses in desperate need of repair. The frequent floods had left their walls stained by mildew and mold.

She had walked only about three blocks when she saw people waiting in line.

"Is this the pizza line?" Sylvia asked a young couple, a shirtless man in his twenties with long brown hair, and an attractive black-haired girl who Sylvia guessed was no more than eighteen. The girl wore tiny shorts that made the bottom portion of her fleshy buttocks visible at the slightest inclination of her upper body.

The girl glanced at Silvia and smiled. "Yes, this is the line," she said in a friendly tone, as the morning sun made her hair shine.

"What's your name?" Silvia asked the girl.

"Elisa," she said.

"Pretty name," said Silvia, and Elisa smiled. "Have you been waiting long?"

"A few minutes," said Elisa, "but judging by where we are, we'll be here for a while."

"Yeah, 'el periodo especial,' señora. That's what this is. We have the Russians to thank for this and of course, our beloved Comandante en Jefe, Fidel Castro," the bohemian-looking man said with sarcasm.

53

The man had bronzed skin and a broken front tooth. The length of his hair and the small cross tattooed on his back suggested to Silvia that he was one of those young men the revolutionaries labeled *elementos antisociales*, a group that, disillusioned by the establishment and the lack of opportunities, had dropped out of society.

Surprised to see him in line, yet fearing to be offensive, Silvia asked the young man, "Did both of you get your coupons from the CDR?"

Proudly, Elisa said, "I did. I volunteered on neighborhood watches every week."

The young man touched his chest with his fingertips and said, "Señora, honestly, do I look like the kind of person who would get a coupon from the CDR?"

Silvia smiled. "Frankly, no, you don't. So, I suppose you don't have one then."

The young man approached Silvia and whispered in her ear. "Yes, I do, but I bought it from a friend of a friend of one of our revolutionary comrades. Fifteen pesos I paid for it."

Silvia shook her head.

Elisa crossed her arms and stared at her boyfriend. "Por favor, Carlos, don't be like that. We should be thankful that the government is giving these coupons to those of us who help the revolution. You know how many people in the world are dying of hunger?"

"You mean us?" he said, turning his head slightly towards her.

Silvia agreed with him but covered her mouth to conceal her amusement.

Pizza Coupons

Elisa angrily pushed her boyfriend out of the line. "I can't stand you sometimes!" she said.

Silvia smiled and shook her head. "You two remind me of when I was young. My husband, Octavio, and I, were always on opposite sides when it came to politics, except towards the end." Silvia inhaled and then exhaled slowly.

She thought about Octavio, forty years earlier, at the steps of the University of Havana, where they first met. She remembered the way he kissed her hand and told her how beautiful she was. And she had indeed been beautiful, with thick, brown hair falling gracefully on her shoulders and undulating as she walked up the steps of the university.

Elisa glanced at Silvia with a concerned expression and said,

"When did he die?"

"Three months ago, a heart attack. Now, it's just me."

"No sons or daughters?" asked Elisa.

Silvia didn't answer immediately. She was distracted by a family, a couple with two little dark-haired girls, who walked across the street with small pizzas folded in white napkins. Then her eyes remained lost somewhere in the distance, beyond a tall *framboyán* tree with orange flowers in full bloom and beyond the porches of unpainted houses that lined the street. Finally, she recalled Elisa's question and took a deep breath.

"Two boys. They left Cuba on a raft," she said.

"I'm sorry, señora," Elisa said.

"Shit, I wish I had left on a raft," mumbled her boyfriend.

Elisa stared at him with her brown eyes wide and whispered, "Are you crazy? Are you trying to get us in trouble? Shut up! Do you want to go to jail for talking like that?" She bit her nails nervously and shook her head.

An old man arrived at the line and stood behind Silvia. The man, who wore a sleeveless t-shirt and had saggy, wrinkled arms, asked her, "Is this the pizza line?"

"Yes," Silvia responded. "And by the way, comrade, I'm holding a spot for my friend, Marta, and her husband."

He shrugged and said, "Fine."

Silvia continued to talk with the couple in front of her for a while. She asked them where they lived and whether they had brothers and sisters, anything to make the time go by. She tried to talk to the old man behind her a couple of times, but he didn't seem interested. She asked him questions like *where do you live* or made comments like *the sun is hot today* but he shrugged or simply ignored her. She gave up and continued to talk to the young couple, who by now had gotten over their spat.

As the day advanced, the temperature rose. Silvia consulted her watch several times and protected herself from the sun with a white umbrella, sent to her by one of her cousins who lived in Miami.

The second time she reminded the old man behind her about Marta and her husband, she noticed his increasing frustration, the way he rolled his eyes and shook his head but did not respond. Behind him, the line had grown so much that Silvia could not see where it ended. People were covered with sweat, making their skin shiny and their hair turn wet and clumpy. Silvia's white blouse was sticking to her back, and she had drunk all the water from the plastic bottle in her purse. Her legs were sore and her energy had evaporated. She rubbed her cheeks, adjusted her eyeglasses, and pulled her hair away from her face as drops of perspiration fell down her neck. Behind her people were starting to become restless, and someone yelled, "Is this damn line going to move?" Others echoed this sentiment, but the line hardly moved.

When she consulted her watch again it was almost two. She told the old man behind her: "My friends should be here any time now."

He evidenced his frustration by the anger in his eyes, and the way he shrank his eyebrows closer together and gesticulated with his hands as he spoke.

"Chica, your friends will have to go to the end of the line when they get here," he yelled, as his face reddened. "I'm hungry as hell. I've been standing in this stupid line for hours. So forget it!"

"Please comrade, be considerate. My poor friend broke her leg. Can you have some compassion?" said Sylvia turning her hands, palms up, fingers stretched forward. The young couple in front of her, who had been hugging and kissing, turned around.

"Why do you have to be like that with the poor woman?" Elisa asked the old man. Then, without waiting for his response, she looked at Silvia and added, "Your friends can get in front of me when they get here."

"Thank you. That's so nice of you," said Silvia.

The old man stared at Silvia angrily. He turned around, behind him, noticing the long line that covered most of the sidewalk and stretched as far as the eye could see, and yelled into the crowd, "Can you believe this woman? She wants to hold a spot for her friends! And who knows how many friends she's bringing." He said the last sentence waving his right arm in the air.

"No! Forget it," several people yelled.

"To the end of the line," said another man.

Silvia shook her head. Of late, when she felt as lonely and helpless as she did then, she would talk to her husband silently and tell him how much she missed him.

She considered going home, but when she saw the people passing by with their pizzas and compared that option to the piece of old bread that she would otherwise have to eat, she decided to stay. Besides, she needed something more substantial; she had lost over twenty pounds since her husband's death.

The people in line continued to shout, while she looked down and closed her eyes until the noise faded. Only the tension on their faces remained.

Silvia examined the houses near the pizzeria. People sat on their front porches fanning themselves and watching the crowd. She concluded that they had most likely already eaten their pizzas. She glanced at the man behind her, who at the time was not paying attention to the front of the line, but seemed distracted looking at the people gathered across the street.

Pizza Coupons

"Oiga. Look. I'm just going to walk a few steps to that house over there and ask for a glass of water. I also need to use the bathroom. I'll be back, okay?"

The man rolled his eyes. "Whatever," he said.

"Thank you very much," she said. Then turning to Elisa, Silvia added, "I'll be right back."

"Si, señora. I'll watch your spot," Elisa said, staring at the old man with anger.

Silvia crossed the street and rushed to the front porch of one of the houses, which seemed to have forgotten better days. There, an elderly couple sat on green rocking chairs and drank café from small, white metal cups.

"I'm sorry to bother you. I've been in line for hours. I'm very thirsty and need to use your bathroom. Can I impose?"

The woman smiled. "Sure, come in. You're not the only one who's been here. Come inside," she added.

The old woman left her husband sitting on the porch and led Silvia inside. They entered the small living room, sparsely furnished with a brown sofa and a couple of wooden chairs across from it. In a corner of the room, Silvia noticed a small altar with the Virgin of Charity, and on the walls several black-and-white pictures. The tall front windows were open, but the house felt warm and stuffy. The walls had peeling green paint.

"Did you get your pizza already?" Silvia asked.

"Yes, we got up very early," the woman said.

"I wish I had done the same," answered Silvia.

The woman smiled. "I'll go to the kitchen to get the water. The bathroom is at the end of the house. See that door?" The woman pointed towards the back of the house.

"Thank you. You're very kind," said Silvia, and walked towards the bathroom.

Once inside, she looked at herself in the small mirror above the sink. She looked awful, with damp and clumpy hair and a red, sweaty face.

"Octavio," she said, as she thought about her husband. "All this for a small pizza."

Her mind wandered when she opened the faucet. She recalled the day her sons, eighteen and twenty, left on a raft. She remembered embracing them on the sand a few hours before dawn as three men and two women insisted they hurry; there was no time to lose. She recalled the smell of the ocean, her empty arms.

After that day, Silvia could not stop blaming herself for once believing in the revolution—the revolution that had made their sons, when they were growing up, wish they were tourists because the tourists had new clothes and shoes and ate the food Silvia's family could only buy in their dreams. The revolution that had once kicked her sons out of a hotel lobby because the hotel was only for tourists. Her husband had recognized its flaws since its early years, when the government had begun to nationalize businesses and when entire families had left it all behind and moved abroad. She had argued with him, assured him that the revolution would benefit the people. But now she realized how little she had known then, and how naïve she must have appeared to her husband.

When her children left, like hundreds of other young people did, she concluded that the revolution would never produce positive changes in her country. It had been destined to fail from the start. Lost in her thoughts, saddened by the years it had taken her to reach this conclusion, she looked down. Then she put her hands together and splashed water on her face. After drying off with a handkerchief from her purse, she walked over to the toilet, which sat next to an old bidet.

When she went back out, the old woman awaited her with a glass of cold water. Silvia drank it fast and the woman quickly refilled it.

"Thank you. You're very kind," said Sylvia.

"My pleasure, but you should be careful standing in the sun for so many hours," said the old woman.

"Señora, what can I do? When you're hungry, you're hungry."

"Don't you have any family here?" she asked.

"No. My sons left Cuba, my husband died three months ago, my brothers and sisters died from old age, and I don't want to leave. Somebody has to care for the dead, don't you think?"

The woman nodded. "Yes, somebody has to," she said. "I wonder what will happen when we're also gone. Who will watch the dead then?"

"We can only worry about the things we can control, señora," said Silvia.

The woman nodded, and moments later, Silvia thanked her again and left.

When she returned to the line, she noticed that it had moved a few steps. She attempted to take her place, but the old man had taken it over and now stood very close to the young couple.

The man ignored Silvia's presence as she patiently waited for him to notice her. When she realized that he wasn't going to acknowledge her, she nudged him.

"I'm back. Thank you for keeping my spot," Silvia said.

The man turned to her, took a deep breath, and reluctantly stepped back.

"Thank you, señor. You're very kind," said Silvia.

The man sneered at her and didn't respond, while she pretended to ignore his rudeness.

An hour later, the line had moved almost two blocks. Silvia could now smell the pizza. As she imagined the melting cheese, the tomato sauce and fresh crust, her stomach growled. She pushed it with her fingers, hoping to stop it from making embarrassing noises. Looking down at her sandals, she noticed the swelling of her feet. The joints and muscles in her legs hurt and she was thirsty again.

Suddenly, she looked up and saw the silhouette of a man and a woman approaching in the distance. The woman had a bandaged leg and walked with crutches.

The man and the woman, whom she now identified as José and Marta, scanned the line with their eyes. Silvia happily waved at them and yelled, "I'm here."

The old man behind Silvia stared at her angrily and said, "I already told you that no one is getting in front of me."

Silvia began to bite her nails as she gazed into the distance. When it became clear to her that Marta and José had not seen her yet, she closed her umbrella and began to wave her hand and the umbrella in the air until Marta saw her and waved back. Marta then began the difficult walk in Silvia's direction, accompanied by her husband, stopping several times to catch her breath. When the couple arrived at last, Silvia first embraced Marta and then patted José on the back. Marta's plump face was shiny from sweat, and she was breathing heavily.

"How're you doing?" Silvia asked Marta.

"Exhausted," Marta said, after catching her breath. "But you can see for yourself," she added, pointing at the bandaged leg.

"Broken?"

"Damaged some ligaments."

The old man behind Silvia, feeling ignored, reminded her in a loud, agitated voice, "Señora, I'm not going to repeat this again. No one is getting in front of me. You hear me?" Blood rushed up to the man's face and the veins swelled at his temples.

Marta gave Silvia a confused look while José stared at the man like an angry bull.

"What are you looking at?" asked the old man.

"You better treat the lady like what she is or you will have to deal with me, you hear?" said José, pointing with his index finger to the middle of the man's chest. He then lifted his chin and stepped closer. José and the old man were about the same age, but José was much heavier and had broad shoulders. His angry expression, his mustache, and his big gut made him look intimidating. The other people in line watched with interest.

Marta secured one of the crutches between her body and her upper arm, grabbed her husband's hand and said, "José, let's go home. My leg hurts, and I don't think I can wait in my condition anyway."

José stared again at the old man, who this time averted his eyes.

"Fine, chica, let's go," José said, raising his arms in surrender. "I don't need this damn pizza anyway."

Marta shrugged, looking as disappointed as she felt, and glanced at Silvia. "I'll see you later," said Marta.

Silvia embraced her friend, kissed her on her cheek, and whispered in her ear, "I'm so sorry."

Marta glanced at her and smiled. "Don't worry about me. I'll be fine," she said.

José and his wife slowly walked away, Marta limping and trying to avoid putting weight on her wrapped leg, José assisting her the best he could. Silvia's eyes focused on them, watching as they stopped frequently for Marta to catch her breath. When at last the couple had disappeared in the distance, Silvia looked at Elisa, who glared at the old man with a furrowed brow.

Silvia looked down, her disappointment etched on her face, and closed her eyes. *How long am I going to have to live like this, Octavio? How long?* she thought.

She ignored the old man after that.

The line kept moving. Now that there were only four or five people in front of her, Silvia's anticipation grew. She was salivating, her stomach aching from the acid buildup, her feet more swollen. She was exhausted.

Pizza Coupons

Five more minutes passed and she had only the young couple in front of her. Soon—she thought—she would be eating a delicious slice of pizza, and the imagined flavor of the melted cheese comforted her. She was a couple of steps from the entrance and the smell of freshly-baked crust, sauce, and cheese inundated her senses.

A man dressed in a white, short-sleeved shirt and blue pants came out of the pizzeria.

"I need everyone to listen carefully," he yelled.

The people at the front of the line gathered around him and so did those behind them, widening the circle around the man in the white shirt. People pushed and shoved each other, encircling Silvia, who lost her balance and had to hold on to Elisa and her boyfriend as a sea of people grew around them.

"Listen very carefully everyone," he said.

Pearls of sweat rolled down Sylvia's face and the anticipation of the people grew.

"I'm very sorry to tell you this," he said first. And before he said anything else, the uncomfortable movement of the people and the indignant looks spread like a virus. And then, the critical words came. "But the electricity just went off. It will be several hours before it comes back. There won't be any more pizza today."

"What you do mean there's no more pizza?" several people yelled.

"That's bullshit," a few people shouted.

Discontent ruled each face in the crowd. Irritation flared as angry voices shouted at the man.

Silvia just stood there in disbelief. Her blood rushed to her head and her heart beat faster, as she repeated those words to herself: *There won't be any more pizza.* People kept pushing her in various directions. She was disappearing within the outraged crowd—and inside her head—as she tried to connect those words to her reality. Silvia felt very dizzy, and her skin was clammy.

She tried to fight her way out of the mob. Everything was spinning, the faces around her were becoming blurred. Her legs weakened. She removed her glasses and dropped them on the street while she covered her face with her hands, many thoughts and images rushing through her mind. She saw a tear rolling down her youngest son's face, as he said good-bye to her on the sand on the day he left. She saw her husband kissing her on her cheek by the steps of the University of Havana, and moments later, the image of him in a casket crossed her mind. She saw her friends, Marta and José, walking away because hunger had turned the old man and the other people in the line into animals; she saw herself standing on the street alone, no longer a mother, no longer a wife, no longer herself.

Her sudden scream paralyzed everyone, a scream that would slowly drown in her tears. She fell down to her knees, and the people around her stepped back in a wide circle. She leaned forward and hit the pavement with her fists, her glossy eyes gazing absently at the crowd, her sadness falling on the asphalt.

People watched her in stunned silence as she wept.

Carnaval in Havana

Blacks, mulattos, and whites dance,
as drums erase the hunger of ration cards.

Rum and beer roam the streets
altering minds.

Ghosts of firing squad victims
awake, among lust and sweat.

No saints sleeping tonight.

Listen to the *conga* music
of Havana's *carnaval*.

Watch the dancing
men and women in miraculous trance.

Floats of laughter mask the tears.
Lights and music bring the monstrous night . . .
alive.

Abuela's Yellow Rice and Chicken

Steamy, with red peppers
mixed in a festive array.

Clumpy, the way I like it,
made with beer to enhance the flavor.

I can smell it from the door
when I arrive at her house in *Marianao*.

"Serve me a plate, *Abuela*. Quickly.
I haven't eaten since this morning."

She does.

Where does she get the chicken? I wonder.

Mother says we are only entitled
to buy six ounces per person, per month.

I ask her.

Abuela's Yellow Rice and Chicken

"I trade the roses in my garden for chicken,"
she says.

She smiles and watches me eat
her concoction.

Old House on Zapote Street

Zapote Street never knew the house's
sorrow, for it kept its desolation inside,
like a splinter buried deep into the flesh.

Memories sustained its cracking ceilings,
recollections of colonial times,
dictatorships, and revolutions.

The generations who lived inside
knew the truth. They *knew* the lies,
the endless struggle, liberties lost.

Meanwhile, children grew in the silence
of a secret life, as people worked,
as people died.

Hush!
These walls can hear your thoughts
but can't block the noise
of a collapsed foundation.

A Cuban Woman's Hopes

Alicia waits in line at the *bodega*
with her ration card in hand.
She has the patience of one hundred virgins.
She knows, hopes, good times will come.

Men stare. They are not shy.
The figure of a pretty woman is all
they have to keep their mind away
from their dismal existence.

Her strapless top betrays her flaccid breasts.
Her legs know the broken sidewalks;
her limbs are tough and strong, ready
for whatever journey they must endure.

And when she buys her quota,
the ration of rice and beans, she knows
it will not last a month, but she will invent,

71

A Cuban Woman's Hopes

like she has done *so* many times.

Alicia walks home, radiant as the wind
and the summer sun, not knowing
the scales at the *bodega* have been altered,
not knowing how fast her food will evaporate.

Still, she hopes. One day . . .
good times will come!

The Raft

On the day Orlando went home after having fulfilled a five-year sentence for conducting "antirevolutionary" activities, he knew his days in Cuba had to be numbered. And now, six months later, here he was somewhat recovered from his days in the darkness of his cell, his body no longer skin and bones. He had gained twenty pounds thanks to the purchases of garbanzo beans and rice in the black market that Nadia, his girlfriend, had procured, but jail had aged him beyond his thirty-five years.

Now, all the conditions were ready: the raft, the food and water, an old compass, a lantern, a blank journal and a pen. These last two items were not needed for the journey; they were key elements of his passion for writing, to be used to document his trip to the United States. That was his plan.

"Orlando, please take care of Nadia and Luisito," said his sixty-five year-old mother-in-law, Luisa, as she embraced her daughter and her grandson.

The Raft

Luisa wore a sleeveless, light-blue house dress that revealed her tan, thin, wrinkled arms. She had more facial wrinkles than most women her age. Orlando thought that her preoccupations with her family were to blame. Both of her sons had left Cuba on rafts, one losing his life in the treacherous journey.

And now, her only daughter and grandson were following their footsteps. She had told her daughter many times to leave Luisito behind, to not risk a child's life to the whims of an unforgiving sea, but she would not listen, and Luisa and her husband were already too old for such a dangerous journey.

Luisa realized this would be the last time she'd see her daughter, as the process to obtain legal residency and citizenship in the United States, which would allow her daughter to claim Luisa and her husband could take years. Luisa's arms were not ready to lose another child to the luring lights of the North.

They all stood on the sand near the sea guarded by heavy shrubbery and palm trees. The moon was out but clouds were moving in. About a dozen neighbors surrounded the family: shirtless men and women in house dresses, or a pair of shorts and sleeveless tops, all looking at those who were departing with curious eyes.

"Don't worry so much. You know I'll take care of them," said Orlando.

And how couldn't he? Nadia was his soul mate, the woman who had faithfully waited for him during the years he spent in jail.

They all stood on the soft sand beneath the dawn sky, only a few feet from the shore and the raft. The summer breeze coming from the sea brushed their faces and made the palm trees dance. Luisito, wearing a pair of beige shorts, a white shirt and brown sandals, looked down at the sand and kicked it nervously with his foot, lifting some into the air and over his grandmother's white sandals.

"Stop kicking the sand," said his mother. Nadia was thin like her mother and had shoulder-length thick, black hair.

"Let him be a child," said Luisa.

Nadia shook her head.

"You spoil him too much, *mami*."

Luisa looked at her with a mixture of pride and not-well-concealed sadness and caressed her daughter's fair and flawless face.

"I'll miss you, *mamá*," Nadia said wiping a tear from her face. "Tell *papá* not to worry. We'll be fine." Her voice was cracking as she pronounced the last words.

Orlando patted Nadia's back. He had strong arms from the hours he had spent working out after he left the jail to ready himself for the trip. He tried to work out in jail, but the food was not enough, and he did not have the energy. His white short-sleeve T-shirt partially exposed his muscular biceps.

"Come on Orlando! We have to go," yelled one of the men on the raft.

"Let's go my love. We're ready," Orlando said taking a deep breath and gently touching Nadia's shoulder. Then turning to the dozen or so neighbors that surrounded them, he said:

"Thank you for helping us with the raft. I'll miss you all."

One by one, the neighbors embraced Orlando, and the women kissed him on his cheek. They looked at him as if he were a celebrity.

"Oh man, you are so lucky," one of the men said. "When you get to the Yuma, don't forget to write and tell us all about it!"

Nadia kissed her mother on her cheek, a gentle kiss, wet with her tears and Luisa embraced her daughter tightly and whispered in her ear:

"May God and the Virgin accompany you, my child."

Then, Nadia took the hand of her seven-year-old son, waved good-bye to the neighbors, and began to walk away, her steps uncertain over the uneven sand.

Orlando stood by Luisa for a moment and patted her on the back gently.

"Well, go home now, *mi vieja.*" He called her *mi vieja,* my old lady, affectionately. "You need to rest."

She nodded and framed Orlando's shaven face with her cold hands and looked at him with the eyes of a mother. She had seen him grow up as he was the best friend of her youngest son. He was always at her house, always getting in trouble, either by listening to prohibited American music or by expressing his discontent with the government.

When her two sons left Cuba, he had helped fill the void. She loved him as her own child, always dreaming of the day her daughter realized that he was the right man for her.

The Raft

"You take care of yourself and have a safe trip. Come on give me a hug" she said.

They embraced.

"Don't forget to write, you hear?" said Luisa. "Some people leave Cuba and forget those they leave behind."

"I won't forget," he said. "Go home now, okay?"

Luisa nodded and began to saunter away, while Orlando took a deep breath, turned around and headed for the raft.

As he walked towards the shore, he thought about the life he was leaving. Behind him stayed Havana, with all the memories of his childhood years and the journals he left hidden under Luisa's mattress. He hoped to come back for them one day. But when he placed his feet on the raft, he felt that a new door had opened, and all he could think about was the life that awaited him beyond the sea.

Nadia had always told him how much of an idealist he was. His idealism had caused him to be jailed. It made him wait years for the only woman he had ever loved. He and Nadia had been good friends since they were children. They used to play hide-and-seek, or other times, they sat on the sidewalk on the corner of Zapote and Serrano streets, under the shade of an almond tree, and crushed the fruit that fell from it with rocks. He had a crush on her since then that evolved into something more powerful. Years later when she fell in love with someone else, he hoped that one day she'd realize she had married the wrong man.

And that moment eventually arrived. The truth faced her only six months after her son was born. Nadia had left her job at the electric company earlier than usual that afternoon, and as soon as she opened the door of her one-bedroom apartment, she heard her son crying inconsolably. She threw her black purse on top of her faded floral fabric sofa and rushed to her bedroom with a look of preoccupation. When she entered, her world crumbled. Her husband lied in bed on top of the white sheets Nadia had purchased in the black market, an undressed bleached blond woman sat on top of his mid-section, her knees on either side of him, her body thrusting against his, as they both moaned with pleasure. Meanwhile, the baby cried in his crib, only a few feet away from the bed. Her normally pleasant demeanor quickly transformed, her face contorting with a mixture of rage and sadness.

"How dare you?" she screamed at her husband, as she rushed towards the woman, grabbed her by her hair and pulled her off of him. The back of the woman's upper body reached the tiled white floor first. When she was face up on the cold floor trying to free her hair from Nadia's grasp, Nadia held on to it and pulled it as hard as she could, until the woman's hair was practically cutting her left hand. She then slapped her with her free hand.

"You inconsiderate whore! Not only do you decide to sleep with a married man but with my son in the room? What kind of animal are you?"

The woman tried to block Nadia's punches, but when she could not, she scratched her with her long nails and pulled her hair, but Nadia could not feel anything. Her eyes were full of tears, and her adrenaline kept flowing as she sat on top of her torso and slapped her face repeatedly.

"This will teach you not to screw with a married man!"

Her husband jumped off the bed and tried to separate the women as the blonde yelled: "You lied to me! You told me you were divorced!"

It took a moment for Nadia to react to her words.

"I did not know he was married. I swear!" The woman said.

Nadia stopped hitting her and slowly, like possessed, she turned to her husband and stared at his naked body that was still showing evidence of his lust for his lover.

"Divorced? Is that what you told her?" Her husband stepped back and placed the palms of his hands up as he said, "Let me explain!"

Like a tigress, she got off the woman, charged towards him and slapped him on the face repeatedly.

"Is that you what you said?" she asked him.

While she fought him, he tried to restrain her, but the blonde got off the floor and started pulling his hair from behind.

"You lied to me!" the blond woman shouted.

"Leave me alone, you bitch!" he said, as he turned his head slightly in the direction of his lover, who was standing behind him burying her nails into his back with one hand and pulling his hair with the other.

The baby was inconsolable. Nadia finally came to her senses and looked at her husband with a mixture of sadness and disgust. She stopped hitting him, lifted her baby from the crib and rocked him in her arms.

"Everything is okay my love," she told her son.

She then raised her eyes and looked at her husband one last time. There was nothing she could tell him that her eyes did not convey. She headed for the door with her son in her arms and never returned. Sometime later, as she cried on Orlando's shoulder while he caressed her long, black hair she would realize what she should had known much sooner.

Nadia had divorced her husband, and she and Orlando took refuge on each other's arms when they needed it the most. Now, nothing could separate them. They would discover freedom together.

"Orlando, I need you to help me, man. What are you waiting for?" someone said.

Orlando turned around. It was Tony, a skinny twenty-year old with long, brown hair tied on a ponytail, who was in knee-deep water trying to push the raft against the waves to take it deeper into the sea. Orlando got off the raft and helped him push it until the water reached up to their necks. Then they jumped back in, aided by the people inside.

"This is it everyone!" Tony whispered. "We need to stay quiet now and hope the Cuban coastguards don't catch us."

"If they do, we may never see the light of day again," said Orlando pensively.

The Raft

"Come on people. We have to remain positive," said Katy, Tony's girlfriend. "You know what they say. Negative thoughts attract negative things."

Katy was red-haired, thin woman, a gymnast and a waitress, strong, outgoing, and optimistic. She had turned twenty the day before. She had struggled with the idea of telling her parents she was leaving Cuba and ultimately decided that it would be better if they learned about it when she arrived to the United States. She did not want them to worry and made up a story that even she had a hard time believing: she was working late because a new delegation from Venezuela was visiting Cuba and she was being paid extra money to work the event. The delegation would be in Cuba for two days, so she would have to sleep at one of her coworkers' apartment during that time. She did not think her parents suspected anything.

"I'll say a prayer to the Virgin of Charity," said Nadia. "I have a small statute of her in my purse. She will protect us."

Nadia's parents were Catholic and she had been taught to believe in God and in a plethora of virgins and saints, like Santa Barbara, San Lázaro, and the Virgin of Charity. The latter was the patron saint of Cuba. Nadia had grown up watching a larger version adorn her bedroom. The virgin wore a beautiful blue gown and held a child in her arms. Beneath her, men in a boat prayed to her for their safety, as they battled the rough seas. Nadia's aunt had given her the small statute during one of her visits from Tampa. Nadia touched the virgin, closed her eyes, and began to pray.

Orlando looked towards the coast. "We are okay for now but we should hurry," he said.

Orlando and Tony rowed, each one sitting on opposite sides of the raft, while the boy sat next to his mother. Katy secured one of the bags of food with a rope.

"When one of you gets tired, I can take over," said Rogelio, a skinny man with a full head of white hair and sunken cheeks.

Rogelio had been the designer and builder of the raft. He had worked on it for months, while Orlando, Tony, Nadia, and Katy procured the materials needed: the inner tubes, the wood, canvases, and rope. Each one of them had contributed to purchasing the food required for the journey in the illegal market because the allotted food rations that the government allowed them to purchase through the ration cards were hardly enough to satisfy their hunger on a daily basis. It was Rogelio who had named the raft. He named it Dalia, like his daughter who was waiting for him in Miami.

"Don't worry about anything, Rogelio. We'll handle it. You just need to watch the compass with that flashlight once in a while and make sure we are heading north," Tony, the youngest of the three men, said.

Everyone remained quiet after that, and all the rafters could hear was the splashing sound of the ores against the water and the raft rising above the waves and then slamming the sea, as it dropped like a toy in a void of darkness. Orlando turned his head around a few times to watch the coastline illuminated by yellow lights. Each time, the lights seemed smaller and dimmer until, after a long while, they completely vanished in the distance, and all he could see was the dark waters that surrounded the raft.

Orlando looked at Nadia. Luisito was now sitting on her lap, and she had her arms around him. Orlando liked the way she looked, her long, black hair held up in a ponytail, illuminated by the moon, her brown eyes sadly watching the foamy waves. She lifted her head and her eyes met his. Realizing he had been looking at her for some time, she smiled.

"Are you thirsty?" Nadia asked Orlando.

"No, I'm fine."

Once again, everyone stayed quiet for a long while until the old man broke the silence, "Orlando, Luis! What's that over there?" he said as in pointed somewhere in the distance.

Orlando looked in the direction the old man was pointing and noticed a light.

"It could be one of the Cuban coastguards," said Tony.

"Are they coming towards us?" asked Rogelio.

Tony didn't answer. Orlando kept looking in the direction of the light and finally said, "I can't tell."

"What do we do?" asked Katy.

"I don't know. But we can't afford to get caught," said Orlando.

Orlando and Tony rowed faster, although Orlando knew that if it was a coastguard, there was little they could do, not if they wanted to make their lives difficult. The wind was starting to pick up. Orlando noticed that a thick cloud had blocked the moon. Maybe now, it would be more difficult for the coastguard to spot them.

"Can you tell if they are coming towards us?" asked Orlando.

"I don't think so," said Nadia. "The lights are not getting any brighter."

"Maybe it's a fishing boat," said Rogelio.

Orlando kept rowing. Occasionally, he would glance at the light. Was it getting any closer? He decided not to look at it anymore. Moments later, as if fighting against his self-imposed restriction, he found himself lifting his eyes. He knew it was pointless. If it were coming from a coastguard boat, he would not be able to escape anyway. His heart was beating faster, and he felt a knot in his stomach.

"Would you like some water, Orlando? You look tired," whispered Nadia trying to keep the noise down.

"Sure, thanks."

Nadia retrieved a plastic bottle from a sac and gave it to him, and he brought it to his lips. The cool liquid felt good on his throat and calmed him, but he didn't want to drink too much. After all, he didn't know how long they would be at sea. He needed to save the supplies.

In an effort to forget the light he had seen, he allowed his mind to drift while he stared at the black waters and rowed. He recalled the day he was arrested for participating in an antirevolutionary meeting and distributing anticommunist leaflets.

The night after the meeting, armed men dressed in gray uniforms stormed into the house he shared with his parents. He was twenty-two then. At first, the men went into his parents' bedroom.

"Where is he?" one of the men asked.

He heard his mother respond with a question, "Who?" There was fear in her voice.

"Orlando Rivera."

"What do you want him for? He didn't do anything," his father said.

"We have orders to take him with us."

Orlando got up and put on his shirt calmly. Seconds later, the men came into his room.

"Are you Orlando?" a short, bald officer asked him.

"Yes," said Orlando.

"You're coming with us," said the officer.

"Why?"

"Antirevolutionary activity. Let's go."

Orlando remembered breathing faster. He was a writer and a thinker, and restricting his writings was like placing his brain on a leash and it made him feel like he was drowning. As he went out of his house, escorted by government officials, he began to yell so that everyone could hear him, "You see this? I'm being taken out of my home for expressing myself. Long live freedom! Freedom or death."

The men began to hit him on the head with their sticks to silence him, but he kept yelling "freedom" until his words collapsed behind the green door of the government vehicle that waited outside.

Tony said something to Orlando that interrupted his thoughts, but he could not hear what it was. Orlando giggled to himself and said in a low tone of voice. "Now we have the freedom to die."

"What did you say?" said Nadia.

"Nothing."

Orlando looked at the boy. He had fallen asleep on his mother's lap. At that moment, he wished he had the child's innocence.

Orlando's muscles hurt from rowing. He stopped for a moment and crossed his arms to massage his shoulders with his fingers.

"Let me row," Rogelio said.

"I can relieve Tony," said Nadia.

"I'll do it. You have to take care of Luisito." Katy got up, grabbed Tony's hands and forced him to stop rowing.

"Fine, you win," he said.

Rogelio got up and balanced himself on the raft until he reached Orlando.

"Come on. Get out of there. Here, you take the compass now."

Orlando listened. Exhausted, he sat next to Nadia and looked in the direction of the light. He could not see it anymore.

"It's gone!" he announced with jubilation.

"And you just noticed?" said Tony laughing. "Where have you been for the last twenty minutes? Oh, that's right. The intellectual was thinking."

"If you keep it, I'll show you what this intellectual can do," said Orlando.

"Hey, young men," said Rogelio. "More order here. The last thing we need is a fight between the two of you."

"Nobody is fighting, Rogelio," said Katy. "They're playing around, right Tony?"

Tony looked at his girlfriend, smirked, and shook his head. "Sure, we're playing."

Trying to change the topic, Nadia asked, "How long before we get to international waters?"

Orlando looked at his watch. "It's supposed to be twelve nautical miles from where we left, more or less. I heard someone say, it could take several hours if we do not have any major complications. But it's hard to know for sure."

Tony rubbed his hands and his eyes lit up as he said:

"The first thing I'm gonna do when I get to Miami is to buy a big mango milkshake and a huge pizza with chorizo and seafood."

"The first thing you're gonna to do when you get to Miami is take a shower," said Rogelio.

Everyone laughed. It was as if the mentioning of the international waters had a calming effect. Luisito was still asleep. His grandmother, Luisa, had secretly placed half of a "*meprobomato*" on his milk to relax him and make him sleepy.

"Why are you going to the States, old man?" Orlando asked Rogelio.

Rogelio scratched his head. "My daughter lives there. I haven't seen her in fifteen years. My wife, she passed away two months ago," he lowered his head.

"Sorry old man," said Tony.

Rogelio stayed quiet for a moment, then suddenly, he lifted his head, as if something had occurred to him and looked in Tony's direction moving his index finger from side to side like windshield wipers.

"But don't you think that I plan to be a burden. I don't want to live off anyone. I know how to make furniture and will find a job doing that. I'm very good at it. What about you?"

Tony laughed and said:

"I'm a rock singer. Lenny Kravitz, Santana, Kiss, you name it. I can do it all. I also play the electric guitar. Right, Katy?"

Tony leaned over and kissed Katy on her lips. She stopped rowing and pushed him away.

"Stop it. Don't you see I'm busy?"She asked.

"Well, am I good or not?" asked Tony.

"Yeah, you're pretty good. Happy?"

"What about you Orlando. I mean I know you are a writer, but you probably won't make a living writing. What else can you do?"

"I used to be a programmer before I went to jail. When I got out, I became a waiter. I realized that working for the tourists I could make more than double the amount I was making as a programmer."

"That's Cuba for you, my friend," said Tony. "We have the best educated prostitutes, cab drivers, and waiters in the world."

There was a long silence again. Katy and Rogelio rowed as fast as their arms allowed them, as if they were in a competition.

"You two are going to lose your arms if you keep rowing like that," said Tony, they ignored his remarks.

The Raft

Katy had strong arms and legs from her years as a gymnast. In comparison, Nadia looked fragile and in need for protection. Orlando brought Nadia closer to him, kissed her on her cheek and then whispered, "I love you." She smiled.

He then consulted the watch that his sister, who lived in the United States, had sent him as a gift. He turned on its light and noticed it was almost three. It was still very dark and thick clouds covered the sky. Orlando yawned then rested his head on Nadia's shoulder. He dozed off for some time, but the increasing rocking movement of the raft awoke him.

Now, the wind was pounding everyone's faces and played with the hair of the two women as they tried to keep it off their faces. Far away from the shore now, the raft thrashed around frantically against relentless and furious waves and clouds moved fast in the sky.

He rubbed his face and looked at the horizon. "A storm is approaching."

"But I thought the weather was supposed to be good?" said Nadia.

"Come on Nadia. And you trust our beloved meteorologists?" asked Tony.

"Will you stop with your sarcasm?" said Katy. "You're getting on my nerves!"

"Rogelio, do you think this raft will survive a storm?" asked Nadia.

"We worked hard on building it," said Rogelio. He was breathing heavily as he rowed. "You see all the wood tied together with rope, the plastic 55 gallon-tanks around it, and the inner tubes? That's quality."

"That's right, *viejo*. This raft is a product of Cuban ingenuity at its best. It won't sink," said Tony.

"You know what, Tony?" yelled Katy. "Maybe if you had to row, you wouldn't talk so much. I'm tired. You take over."

"*Viejo*, Katy is right. Let's switch," said Orlando not waiting for him to respond. He shuffled closer to Rogelio and took over the row. Katy was not as careful, still upset with Tony about his sarcasm. She stood without thinking and tried to gain balance, but a big wave splashed the raft angrily, and before anyone could do anything, Katy's body tumbled into the dark sea and disappeared.

"Oh my God!" yelled Nadia. "Somebody do something!"

"Give me the flashlight, *viejo*. Hurry!" yelled Tony. Desperately, Tony looked outside the raft for any signs of Katy.

"Katy!" he screamed. Tony began to unbutton his shirt.

"What are you doing?" said Rogelio.

"Going after her! What else?"

Rogelio grabbed Tony's arm. "Don't you understand? The seas are too rough and dark. She's gone. You won't be able to find her. I'm sorry."

"I can't let her drown. Katy! Katy!" Tony yelled while Rogelio tried to restrain him.

"She's gone!" Orlando replied trying to conceal the horror on his face.

The waves kept pounding the raft violently, and now the rain was falling hard against their bodies, without giving anyone time to recover. Rogelio, sickened by the motion of the sea, began to vomit. Nadia, still shaken by Katy's disappearance, was too focused on scanning her surroundings to worry about him.

"Katy!" she yelled, her voice cracking. "Please answer me."

"Katy!" yelled Orlando trying to share Nadia's optimism, and taking the flashlight from Tony to point it at the dark waters.

When there was no response, Nadia frantically took some of the extra rope that secured the side of the raft and tied it around her and her son. She placed her arms around the boy and held him tight.

"Katy! Please say something," Tony said. He continued to call her name until the tears drowned his words.

The boy opened his eyes and mumbled that he was not feeling well and was cold. Nadia kissed his wet hair and pressed her body against his. "Try to sleep, sweetheart," she whispered.

The rowing had stopped completely now. Orlando looked down, and Tony sobbed quietly, his shirt unbuttoned and wet from the waves and the rain.

"I'm sorry, man," said Orlando.

"Orlando, the waves are getting higher. Rowing will be useless," yelled Rogelio as the rain and the water from the ocean splashed against their bodies.

"You're right. We need to tie ourselves to the raft. Nadia, secure the food and the water!" he yelled.

Nadia reached for the sacs of supplies which were already tied, but she reinforced them by tying more rope around them and to the wood on the bottom of the raft. Luisito's eyes were wide open now and he began to cry.

"I'm not feeling good," he said. "I'm scared."

Nadia embraced him and kissed him on the cheek, as guilt inundated her. "We'll be fine, my love. Don't be scared," she said with tears in her eyes.

Orlando and Rogelio placed ropes around their bodies and tied them to the side of the raft. "Tony, come on, tie yourself!" yelled Rogelio.

"This sucks, *viejo*. We're not gonna make it. We're all going to die!" Tony yelled frantically while he reluctantly obeyed Rogelio.

"No one else is gonna die! Stop talking like that," he said.

"Now, all we can do is to pray to the Virgin of Charity!" said Rogelio with a weakened voice.

Orlando held Nadia and Luisito closer to him. She was trembling.

"We'll be fine, *mi amor*," he said. But he didn't believe his own words. He realized now that the change of weather had converted the raft into a deathtrap.

Nadia glanced at him with her eyes full of tears, then bowed her head and began to pray. Suddenly, a huge wave came and covered the entire raft. For a while, Orlando found himself being dragged underneath the wave. He held his breath until the water receded.

He looked around. The wave had pushed Nadia and her son against the side of the raft. The boy was crying and embracing his mother. Tony was next to them.

The Raft

"Is everyone still here?" Orlando yelled. Everything was dark, and his clothes and hair were drenched.

"We are here," said Nadia.

"Me too, but I think we lost Rogelio!" yelled Tony. Then his eyes wandered and he added, "And a bag of supplies."

"Where's the flashlight? We need to see if Rogelio's out there," yelled Nadia.

"Gone," said Tony.

"Rogelio! Rogelio!" yelled Orlando, but no one answered.

"Rogelio!" yelled Nadia frantically.

A long silence followed, disturbed only by Nadia's and Luisito's sobbing and the sound of the rain and the roaring sea. The raft rocked wildly, sometimes rising above the waves and plunging again into the darkness. Thinking that at any moment, the raft would split into pieces, Orlando's heart began to beat faster. He noticed Nadia embracing her son and holding on to a rope. Luisito screamed in fear each time the raft plunged into the sea, while he desperately held on to wood that kept it together. But even the child, through his behavior, began to accept the gravity of the situation and eventually stopped crying. Only the terror on his face remained.

After a long while of battling the sea and the rain, the rain stopped and the full moon began to reappear in the sky, but the waves were still high due to the high winds.

Everyone remained silent and stared at the sea. Nadia sobbed inconsolably and Orlando looked away to hide the tears that rolled down his face. They were at the mercy of the winds and the waves, and he did not know how long it would take them now to reach international waters.

Nadia wiped her face and a mixture of anger and sadness etched her expression. She furrowed her brow and her voice cracked as she said:

"How are we supposed to make it now, Orlando?"

"Calm down, mi amor. You don't want to upset Luisito. We'll figure it out."

Tony shook his head and laughed.

"You know, Orlando? You really crack me up. You must be the most optimistic man in the world. Look around you, man. What now?"

Orlando began to breath faster. He tensed his body and clenched his fists.

"Man, I'm tired of your sarcasm," he said staring at Tony. "Maybe if you shared just a little bit of my optimism, we wouldn't be in this situation!"

"Oh, so now it's my fault," said Tony placing his right hand on the middle of his chest. "Who the hell was the one with all these dreams about freedom?"

Tony's sarcasm echoed through his words.

"That's all bullshit, man," he said. "I had freedom when I played my guitar, when I sang my tunes. Now, I'm stuck in the middle of this deathtrap, lost my girlfriend. And for what? Even the old man is gone, man. And all he wanted was to see his daughter and make his furniture."

Nadia took a deep breath. Deep down, she agreed with Tony.

"Orlando is right, Tony," she said in support of the man she loved. "We knew what was at risk when we left. But we were willing to pay the price."

Tony's eyes focused on the sea for a while which by now had begun to settle down. He moved his head from side to side.

"This sucks!" Tony said hitting the raft with his fists. "What am I going tell her family now?"

He remained silent for a moment.

"Oh, I know! I know what I'll tell them," he added with sarcasm. "I'm a piece of shit who didn't protect her."

"This is not your fault. She knew this could happen," said Orlando.

"Forget it, man," said Tony.

* * *

Eight days had passed since the group had left Cuba. All the food and the water were gone. The rafters who remained were just there, drifting to the whims of the sea. A few moments earlier, they had learned what several days at sea, hunger, and dehydration could do to a man, how one starts to see things that are not there.

"Hey guys. There she is!" Tony had said pointing to the horizon. "I see her." His white teeth seemed to shine against his burnt skin.

"Hey, Katy. I'm here! Wait for me," he said.

He waved, smiled and his eyes remained fixated in the distance. Somehow, despite his weakened state, he managed to gain balance and stand.

"Wait for me, Katy," he said again. "See you soon, guys."

And he jumped into the sea.

Those remaining did not have the energy to save him. Moments later, Orlando saw the sharks and blood floating to the surface. The sea creatures were all around them. Orlando closed his eyes and prepared to die. He held Nadia's hand. It was cold. She had stopped talking since her son fainted. He knew the boy was alive because of the faint heart beats, but it would not be long.

Orlando never imagined it would end like this. He was afraid at first, and he knew that as long as he feared for his life, he had a fighting chance. But when he replaced fear with resignation, he realized he was done. Now all that remained was the wait. As a writer, he hoped that their impending death would not be in vain. He only wished that someone could find the raft and read the scribbles he left. He wanted the world to understand, naïve as that sounded. Nadia was not moving any more. He shook her to see if she was still alive, but she did not respond. Orlando was the only one with any conscious thought left. So much silence reigned interrupted only by the sound of the waves. He stayed still, eyes closed, his hand holding Nadia's, and prayed the end would come soon.

Eternity awaited, but then . . .

Orlando could see Nadia swimming on an aqua-green beach, her thin arms arching perfectly in and out of the warm water. He swims after her. Their breathing becomes heavier with each stroke. He catches up with her, grabs her legs and pulls her towards him. She struggles to stay afloat at first, then turns around and reaches for his hands; she pulls her body closer to his, cradles him with her long legs and repeatedly thrusts her body against and away from his, teasing him until neither one of them can stay away. They embrace and her legs remain wrapped around him under the water. His body reacts to hers. She smiles and kisses his wet neck softly, seductively, moving closer and closer to his lips. Her kisses tickle and energize every sensitive part of his body. Their playfulness continues until they consummate their passion under the sun, their only witness. He closes his eyes and his senses enjoy being inundated by hers. She is his paradise. Being there with her *is* living.

But after a while, he can no longer feel her and realizes that what he was seeing and feeling was not real. She was not there, and he was not there. They were lost somewhere between life and death. All the color and beauty disappears, and he moves through a tunnel of darkness as if he had fallen in a black hole. He is dying. He feels himself letting go.

Ahead, a faint light appears, and in no time, it grows brighter, so bright, it blinds him temporarily. Then, he feels the pinch of a needle going into his arm, and liquid runs through his veins, bringing life into him. After a while, he opens his eyes and sees a light illuminating one of his pupils, then the other. He also sees the face of a blond woman who wears a white doctor's coat. She has a badge hanging from her neck he cannot read. He feels dizzy. He tries to talk, but he is still too weak, although his eyes convey his desperation and she seems to notice it.

"If you are concerned about the woman and the boy, they will be fine," the doctor says in Spanish. Her voice sounds to him like the voice of an angel. "A fisherman found you and them. They are safe."

She smiles, and he closes his eyes for a moment, then opens them again.

"One more thing," she says. "I have the journal you tied around your body and read it in case there was information there we could use to treat you. And yes, you are finally free. Welcome to America."

Orlando's eyes filled with tears, while he repeats her words in his mind, over and over again, until he falls asleep.

Between Buckets of Water

In Cuba, the land of rum and *guaguancó* Afro-Cuban music, *Santería*, and sugar cane, lived Maria. The neighbors saw her often, walking on Zapote Street, carrying two plastic buckets filled with water, even on days when water came out of the faucets. Everything was scarce in Havana during the years Fidel Castro remained in power: water, food, clothes, and electricity. The government would shut down the water, sometimes for days, as a conservation measure. Trucks would then come to Zapote Street to deliver it and people, including Maria, stood in line, waiting for their turn to fill their buckets. One day, the pipes at Maria's apartment broke, and with no materials available to fix them, she had to use the water from a neighbor's house for over a year. The times she walked back and forth, carrying her buckets, and the mysterious sorrow in her green eyes made people notice her.

At age twenty-two, she had the subtle beauty of three continents: emerald eyes from her maternal grandfather, who had Spanish and German heritage, and olive skin, revealing the mixture of her father's African and Taíno Indian roots. She wore her long, black hair in an untidy ponytail held back with a rubber band.

Her mother, Tomasa, a heavy, short woman with milky white skin and colored black hair, practiced *Santería*, an Afro-Cuban religion that incorporates elements of Catholicism and involves secret teachings transmitted from generation to generation to priests and priestesses.

Her stepfather, Cayel, a tall man of dark complexion, practiced a more sinister form of *Santería*: black magic. Similar to the white magic side of *Santería*, it involved animal sacrifice, a firm belief in the saints or *orishas*, and food offerings to the saints. An important difference was that it involved a victim. He used it to harm people he disliked. He had no boundaries, and this made his neighbors fearful of him.

Maria took care of her two younger "brothers," although some suspected they were really *her* children. Tomasa was obese, and people would have had a difficult time noticing her pregnancy. The way Maria dressed, with dark clothes that were too big for her, made it impossible to detect any physical changes.

The young woman could hear people whisper when she walked by, speculate about the reasons for the emptiness in her gaze. No one knew what happened behind the doors of her apartment, when Cayel came home late at night. She kept replaying in her mind the first time he sneaked into her bedroom, while her mother slept, the way he touched her and violated her as she remained motionless, petrified by fear, drops of sadness falling on her pillow when he stole her innocence. He told her he would kill her if she said anything, but when her first pregnancy came, and her mother remained silent about her condition, she realized her loneliness. She gave birth to her first child at age seventeen. Two years later, a second child was born, both secretly delivered at home by one of her mother's relatives.

At first, she blamed herself. She thought, that perhaps, the way she dressed provoked him, not that there was anything particularly attractive or revealing about her plain cotton white and yellow dresses.

After he robbed her of her virginity, she began to wear dark and oversized clothes that belonged to her deceased grandmother. But nothing changed. He still came into her bedroom whenever he wished and forced himself on her. If she refused him, he would restrain her and did with her as he pleased, making her wish she were dead. She thought about running away, but she did not want to leave her children alone with her mother and step-father.

The neighbors saw Maria cry often on street corners but, afraid of Cayel, no one dared to ask her why. One day, her crying stopped and dark shadows appeared under her starless eyes. Rumors emerged, fairly accurate ones, but none of the neighbors dared to intervene.

Everyone in the neighborhood despised Cayel, especially after he tried to kill José, a young black man with a good heart and a handsome smile who lived in the neighborhood with his family. José's son had pushed Cayel's during a fight. It wasn't a big deal; both children were only five, but Cayel wanted revenge.

One day, he hid behind a tall tamarind tree in the corner of Zapote and Serrano Streets, and waited for José to return from work. He didn't have to wait long. Once the unsuspecting José walked by, Cayel grabbed him by his white shirt and delivered several blows to his face. He also punched him in the stomach, causing the small-framed José to fall to the ground. Cayel then kicked him savagely, until there was almost no life in him. After this senseless act, the neighbors' fear of Cayel grew. Yet, they pitied Maria, for she was as much a victim of him as José.

Maria worked hard keeping her house clean, finding food offerings for her stepfather's saints, raising the kids, and carrying her buckets of water. People stayed away from her and ignored her, as if she were a ghost. The only person who greeted her regularly was a twelve-year-old girl who lived in a colonial house next to the apartment building where Maria lived. The girl would stand on her front porch when she passed by, and smile or wave at her. One day the girl, whose name was Tania, offered to assist her. Initially, Maria rejected her help, but when Tania insisted, she allowed her to carry one of the buckets.

"What's your name," Tania asked her, her amber eyes looking into hers.

"Maria," she said sadly.

"Like the Virgin," said Tania.

Tania was petite, with fair skin and long brown hair. Despite her thinness, she had strong arms and did not seem to mind the heavy bucket. They walked on a long, narrow, and dark corridor that separated Tania's house from Maria's apartment building, when suddenly Tania asked Maria, "Is Cayel your father?"

That question seemed to take Maria by surprise.

"Why do you ask?"

"I have been writing stories since I was six," said Tania. "I like to watch people to see how they walk and talk, the happiness or sadness in their eyes. You look very sad all the time. If I had my father with me, I would be happy."

"Where is your father?" Maria asked.

"In the Unites States. The government doesn't let my family go there to be with him. He left Cuba when I was three."

"My father is dead," said Maria. "He died when I was five."

"I'm sorry about your father," she said. "I thought we had something in common."

Tania smiled and remained silent for a moment.

"My friends think my father is a traitor for going to the United States," she said, as her smile turned to sadness.

"Do you think he is a traitor?" asked Maria.

"No," the girl said shaking her head.

"Don't worry about what they say then."

Tania put down her bucket and embraced Maria, who reciprocated by caressing her brown hair with one hand, while still holding a bucket with the other.

After passing several apartments, Maria stopped by the penultimate door. They placed the buckets on the floor, and Maria placed the key in the keyhole. Tania nervously watched the dirty door open. In front of them awaited the saints, *San Lazaro, Santa Barbara,* and the *Virgen de la Caridad,* with lit candles and food offerings by their ceramic statues: two stiff-looking bananas and what appeared to be a plate of stale black beans and rice. The Virgin of Charity's statue was particularly beautiful. It was the Cuban version of the Virgin Mary, holding Jesus Christ in her arms. Beneath her, as part of the statue, three men on a boat prayed to the virgin.

A sour odor emanated from the apartment. Tania looked scared as the saints made her recall an incident that had occurred some years earlier. She said good-bye to Maria and quickly walked away.

Tania had feared Maria's mother since she was very young. A relative had sent Tania a brown doll from the United States. Tomasa, Maria's mother, had seen Tania playing with it on her red-tile porch, and her eyes had grown bigger at the thought of using it for one of her rituals.

Tomasa dashed to her apartment and returned waving a twenty-peso bill in between her dirty fingers.

"I'll buy the doll from you," she told Tania.

"No, she's mine," Tania said holding the doll against her chest. "I don't want to sell it."

Tomasa looked at Tania with piercing black eyes that scared her. Suddenly, the brown doll fell from Tania's hands, and when she picked it up, its eyes had rolled back. The girl threw it on the floor and yelled, "What did you do? You broke it!"

Tomasa laughed, placed the twenty pesos in her bosom and sauntered away.

Tania ran inside the house in tears.

"Mom, Tomasa killed my doll! She wanted to buy it, and I wouldn't sell it to her. She killed it!"

Her mother rushed outside and found the doll on the floor. She noticed the white eyes. Afraid that Tomasa had placed a spell on it, she went back inside the house, brought out a brown paper bag, and carefully put the doll inside it. She then threw it in the garbage, and told Tania to stay away from Tomasa.

Tania knew that if her mother learned of the unsolicited help she had given Maria, and that she had accompanied her to her apartment, she would be angry and decided to remain silent about the encounter.

One Saturday, three days after Tania helped Maria, shouting from the hallway next to Tania's house awoke the people in the neighborhood. Moments later, someone knocked on the door at Tania's house.

"Please let me in! Hurry, I'm scared!" a female voice said.

Laura, Tania's mother, peaked out through the peep hole and recognized Maria. She let her in, and quickly shut the door behind her. They could still hear the shouting outside.

"What's wrong, sweetheart?" Laura asked her.

Maria was breathing fast and placed her left hand on her chest. Laura, noticing her nervousness, asked her to sit down.

"Sweetheart," said Laura, "let me bring you some water first. I need you to calm down, and then tell me what happened."

Tania stayed with Maria, while her mother disappeared in the back of the house, only to return moments later with a tall glass of cold water. Maria took a sip and put it down on the wooden coffee table. Laura sat next to her and tapped Maria's back, while Tania fearfully stood in front of them, chewing her index finger.

"Tania, take your fingers out of your mouth," said Laura. "And you, Maria, take a deep breath and tell me what happened."

Maria's eyes filled with tears as she spoke.

"I was bringing my buckets of water to my apartment, when I saw José waving a machete in front of my door, and screaming for my step father to come out. I'm very afraid for the children!" she cried.

Laura made the sign of the cross.

"Oh, *Jesús, Maria y José*," she said. "Do you know why he's looking for him?"

"I think he wants to retaliate for what my step-father did to him the other day," she said. "I don't blame him. I just don't want the children to get hurt!"

Outside, on the street, the indecipherable yelling continued. Suddenly, they heard a group of people chant, "Kill him. Kill him!"

Maria, Laura, and Tania all rushed to the bedroom adjacent to the living room and opened the window. The neighbors had poured into the streets, and watched as José chased Cayel waving a machete.

"Kill him. José, kill him!" some of the neighbors repeated.

Cayel's white shirt was torn, he bled from his arm, and neighbors screamed for his death, as if they had gone mad. The hate and fear that neighbors felt toward Cayel had reached its boiling point.

"Kill him, kill him!" the people chanted.

"Kill him!" yelled Maria from the window.

Laura looked at Maria's face in shock, noticing the mixture of anger and sadness that accompanied her tears.

"I'm sorry," she said.

Laura embraced her.

"No, sweetheart," she said. "You don't have to apologize."

Maria rested her head on Laura's shoulder and wept inconsolably, while Laura patted her on her back with the heartfelt compassion of a mother. Moments later, the yelling from the street made them break their embrace and focus their eyes outside the window. There, Cayel was fighting for his life. And from their window, they saw Jose's machete rise in the air, shining, illuminated by the morning sun, and slash Cayel across his arms and chest.

Cayel stumbled to the ground, while he tried to contain the blood with his hands, but the blood spurted out continuously, rolling down to the concrete. Moments later, Cayel, as if he had seen a ghost, let out a scream and stayed very still.

"Not even his saints can help him now," Maria said in a somber tone, shutting the window and walking towards the living room.

The neighbors returned to their houses quietly. And Cayel bled to death on the streets of Havana without a single soul coming to his rescue.

After Cayel's spirit had left him, Tomasa and her brother walked up to him quietly, lifted his lifeless body, and carried him home.

Later that day, as Tomasa scrubbed the dried blood from the concrete, the neighbors saw Maria again carrying her buckets of water. This time, she walked at a livelier pace. The youth had returned to her expression, her hair was down and combed neatly.

Broken

"Who am I?" Alexis asked himself as he stood shirtless in front of the broken mirror in the small room he shared with his sister.

His dreamy green eyes, his muscular *café con leche* complexion, a smile that lit up the darkest of nights, and the way women flung themselves at him, would have led anyone to believe that he was on top of the world. He measured over six feet, towering over most of his friends on Zapote Street and had achieved a black belt designation in karate. At plain sight, he had everything going for him. Yet, why did he feel so uncomfortable, so miserable in his own skin?

He knew perfectly why. God knows he did! But he had learned to play the game and did what others expected of him, only to regret it later when he laid in bed awake during the long sleepless nights.

Dalia, one of the women he had slept with, told him she was pregnant with his child. At first, he doubted her. Soon after, he spoke to people who knew her and learned she came from a good family. Her father worked as a programmer for the electric company, while her mother stayed home with her children. No one knew Dalia to be the kind of girl who slept around.

He considered himself to be a good judge of character and saw kindness in her eyes. Her bright smile and the caring way she spoke about her parents revealed her inner beauty. Besides, there were few things the neighbors did not know about each other, so when she swore that she was carrying his child, he felt compelled to believe her. The eighteen-year-old had begged him to marry her. But why perpetrate the lie any longer?

He thought Dalia deserved something better, not the fraud he had become. He could no longer hide from himself, but to come clean, to tell everyone the truth, would cost him so much. Was he willing to lose it all? Or should he continue to enable the lie, while he died little by little every day?

A knock on the door distracted him from his thoughts. Earlier that morning, his parents and his little sister had taken a bus to visit a sick relative in Old Havana, leaving the house to himself. He enjoyed the silence and the stillness when everyone was out. He felt safe. No eyes looking through him, no risk of judgment broadcasting its unpleasant face. Now that the silence had been pierced again, the risk reemerged. Before he left the room, he threw an undershirt on as an afterthought; it felt too warm to wear anything else.

He heard someone knocking again.

"I'm coming!" he said mortified.

Broken

When he opened the door, he seemed surprised to see her. Her eyes were red, her lashes clumped together, and her shoulder-length brown hair looked untidy.

"Can I come in?" Dalia asked with a soft voice.

"Sure," he said.

He swung the door open, closed it behind her –to avoid eavesdroppers– and asked her to sit down. Rumors . . . his worst enemy, and one of the few distractions his neighbors had that made them feel more human and better about their own lives.

She sat on the discolored, blue fabric sofa and pulled her pink skirt closer to her knees, in contrast with the way she acted when they first met. That night, affected by the alcohol, the music, his captivating green eyes and musky smell —going against the values her mother had taught her— she publically flirted with him, kissed him passionately on the dimly lit dance floor, and led him to her friend's bedroom. He did what was expected of him.

"Have you been crying?" he asked.

He sat on a dark wooden chair across from her, not knowing what to think or what to say.

"Yes," she said and looked absently at a black and white picture of his parents' wedding on one of the living room's green walls.

"What happened?" he asked.

She turned her head to look at him. They made eye contact, and she nervously tucked her hair behind her ears.

"It's my parents," she said. "They are furious. They want me to have an abortion."

As many times as he had wished that *his* mother had aborted him, the thought of *his* child being aborted horrified him.

"Is that what you want?" he asked her.

Her light brown eyes filled with tears.

"No, I could never do that," she said placing her hand on her puffy belly. "I just don't want my son to be born to an unwed mother."

He remained silent and averted her eyes, while she stared at him as if trying to read his mind.

"Don't you think that you and I . . .?" she said.

He took a deep breath.

"Dalia, we had this conversation before," he said with a serious expression.

"But I think . . . I'm in love with you."

He lifted his head to look at her.

"In love?" he said. His eyebrows knitted close together in confusion. "We just met eight weeks ago."

Dalia and Alexis had lived a couple of blocks away from each other since they were born, and possibly had seen each other playing on the streets as children, but they had never spoken until that night.

"It would not be the first time someone falls in love at first sight," she said.

Alexis focused on the decorations on the tile floor, as he felt a tension pain on his neck. His expression contorted, while he reached for the back of his neck with his left hand to massage it. He then looked at her.

"There are things that I cannot tell you," he said. "But understand this. I'm not the man for you."

As he spoke, her eyes swelled with tears. After a long silence, she could no longer hold back her emotions and started to weep. He gently patted her arm until she calmed down.

"I know, this is my fault," she said, her voice cracking.

She looked down and framed her face with her hands, remaining silent for a moment, her expression distorted with sadness. Then slowly, she raised her head and looked at him.

"I know I was reckless," she said.

Her last words sounded more like a confession than an admission of responsibility.

"I should have never done what I did," she said. "I don't know what happened. You looked so handsome that night. . . You *are* handsome. You awoke something in me, and . . . I just fell for you."

He remained silent. How could he tell her the truth? But in not responding, he felt increasingly worse, like an enabler of her misery.

"I don't know why you think you are not the man for me," she said. "I believe I could make you happy. Don't you like me? Am I not attractive?"

"You are very attractive," he said. "But that is not the problem. There are other issues that I am not ready to discuss with you yet."

Her expression changed suddenly from sadness to determination.

"Alexis, it is difficult for me to ask for help," she said, her eyes piercing his. "But I need you, regardless of whether or not you care about me. If you feel something about this child I carry inside me, you need to help me."

She now had his full attention. Of course he cared. What kind of monster would he be if he did not care about his own child? He was not like some of his friends who impregnated girls and then insisted they have an abortion. He was ready to face the responsibilities of being a father. But that was not the only thing she wanted from him.

"Please marry me," she said. "I beg you. My parents have threatened to kick me out of the house if I don't have an abortion. The only other way they will accept my pregnancy is if I'm married."

He rubbed his face and stayed in silence. Deep down, he understood her. She too was trying to live up to standards others had set up.

"If there is another girl," she said, "I'm willing to look the other way. Please don't abandon me."

Her words touched his heart.

"There is no other girl," he said. "Listen . . . I will help you with money and all the support you need. I will not abandon my child. I just don't think that marrying you is fair to you."

She rested her elbows on her knees and clasped her hands together, resting her chin on them for a moment. She then raised her head and looked at him.

"Let me be the judge of what is fair or not," she said, sounding calm. "If I do not make you happy, you can later walk away, but at least I will not be an unwed mother by the time our child is born."

He stared at the floor. What had he done? He had unwittingly ruined two lives. Was there anything that he could do right? He felt sorry for Dalia.

He took a deep breath and examined his options.

"I cannot promise you the normal life of a husband and wife," he finally said. "Do you understand?"

"I accept whatever terms you give me," she said. "I will never pressure you."

He inhaled deeply, then exhaled, his face contorted with a mixture of frustration and acceptance.

"You don't know what you are getting into, but if this is what you want . . . "

Her eyes lit up. She grabbed his hands in between hers.

"Really? You will marry me?"

"Yes, I will," he said, regretting it the moment he said it, but he knew Dalia did not have many options, his child did not have many options.

"Can I hug you?" she asked. "Like a friend. I promise."

They both stood almost simultaneously, and she gave him a warm embrace.

"Thank you," she said. "Now, we need to tell my parents."

He agreed to speak to her parents the next day. He needed time to gather his thoughts. It was not difficult for him to predict what would happen next. His parents' happiness. Dalia's parents' joy when they learned that their little girl was getting married to someone who worked as bodyguard for a key figure in the Cuban revolution. His friends' congratulations and the surprised looks of those who knew. His little sister's joy when she learned she was going to be an aunt.

As the wedding plans began, his mother insisted on having a church ceremony, but that was the last thing Alexis needed. The Communist Party frowned upon the practice of religion, and he was a member. His mother finally settled for a small civil wedding, followed by a reception at his home: some beers, fruit punch with rum, a cake, and pastries from La Gran Vía Bakery. Fernando, Alexis's father, bold, round-faced, an oversized gut, approached his son during the reception, big smile on his face, and patted him on his back.

"I'm proud of you, son," he told him. "She's a beautiful girl. You really did a good job hiding her from us."

Getting closer to Alexis's ear, he added, "And I was actually starting to worry."

Alexis pressed his lips together in a line and nodded.

"You seem a little nervous," his father said. "It's normal. Should I get you a beer?"

"No, dad. I'm fine. Thank you."

Meanwhile, Alexis's mother, Lily, was glowing with happiness. She wore a cream-colored embroidered dress that her mother had saved from her younger years. Earlier that day, she had a neighbor color her hair light brown. The hairdresser then brushed it and pinned it up elegantly. For the final touch, she sprayed it with a thick layer of hairspray a family member had brought from the United States. She had the confidence of the queen of

England when she mingled with invited guests and family.

And just like that, Alexis became a married man with a baby on the way.

The new couple moved into Dalia's house on Zapote Street. Housing in Cuba was very scarce and it was common for multi-families to live under one roof. Her three-bedroom house had more space than his because her father had built a wooden loft inside, just above the dining room, to accommodate the growing family. Her brother, who shared a room with Dalia before she married Alexis, had moved to the loft. Her parents occupied the third bedroom.

During the couple's first evening alone, Dalia wore an attractive beige, lacey babydoll that an aunt had brought her from the United States, and let her hair down. She tried everything she could to please her husband and make him forget whatever else troubled him. Alexis reacted as he thought he was expected to react. But in order to fulfill his duties as a husband, he closed his eyes and imagined himself in someone else's arms. Afterwards, when she laid in bed satisfied, content to be Alexis's wife, she took his hand, turned her body towards him, and whispered in his ear, "I love you. Thank you for making me the happiest woman in the world."

This was not the life he had promised Dalia. He did not want her to have false expectations about their future. As much as he did not want to hurt her, he could not put his old life on hold, not completely.

A week after he moved in, he began to go out on weekends. He would attend clandestine "ten pesos" parties organized in the interior courtyards of beautiful Havana homes. A different house would be used each time to avoid alerting authorities that, in the late 1970s, frowned upon his lifestyle. He often questioned his urges. He asked himself whether he had been born broken. Only within the walls of those houses he felt at home, he felt whole. Within them, he had fallen in love.

It saddened Dalia to see her husband return late at night, sometimes after having too many drinks, but true to her word, she remained silent. Later, when she thought he slept, she would weep quietly. Feeling sorry for her, he would turn around, embrace her, and she'd fall asleep in his arms. If he could only be what others considered "normal," life would be so much simpler, but the more he lived in two fragmented worlds, the more broken he felt.

His new lover wanted him to end his dual life, but Alexis had promised Dalia to be with her until the birth of his son. He wanted to remain true to his word, even if he could not shut down completely his true self.

One evening, after he finished work, his wife welcomed him with "a special meal." It had been a warm day. The two buses he took to get back home were so full that he was hanging from the rear door during most of the trip. A musty smell emanated from him; he felt filthy. After a quick shower, he sat at the table with Dalia's family, and his eyes lit up when he saw the meal served on wooden plates: black beans, rice, plantains, and pork. He could not recall the last time he saw so much food.

"Where did you get all this?" he asked.

Dalia placed her index finger vertically across her lip and smiled.

"Let me worry about that. You worry about eating," she said.

"You are not going to get me in trouble, are you?" he asked turning his head slightly. "The last thing I need is for police to come to the house and take my pregnant wife to jail for buying food in the illegal market. I know all this did not come from our rations."

Dalia, her parents, grandparents and little brother all laughed.

The family talked about a number of subjects during their meal: the smaller rations, the frequent blackouts, and the man in the neighborhood who sold guava marmalade with guavas he bought on the illegal market. Dalia's mother had purchased a jar for desert.

After dinner, as Alexis helped her clear the table, Dalia announced from the kitchen where she washed the dishes:

"I need you to clear your Saturday evening. Your parents invited us to dinner."

He brought his eyebrows closer together.

"But I had plans!" he said mortified.

She stuck her head out of the kitchen.

"They have everything planned, even invited some family members," she said.

He shook his head. He wanted to call his parents and make them cancel the dinner, but he knew them well. They would not take no for an answer. Besides, the eyes of Dalia's family were all on him.

. Later that evening, it angered Alexis's lover to learn that he would not be able to make their date. They argued, but Alexis knew all would be forgotten by the following week. He felt manipulated by his parents and everyone else around him.

That weekend, he thanked his mother for organizing the dinner but asked her not to arrange any gatherings without clearing them with him first.

"Is everything ok?" she asked.

"Yes," he answered.

The smirk on his mother's face and her distrustful and sad look made him realize that she had read beyond his dismissive response.

* * *

During the months Alexis lived with Dalia, her generosity, her insistence in pleasing him, led Alexis to become very fond of her, so much so that sometimes he would bring her home her favorite deserts from La Gran Vía Bakery. They had become good friends, although their love life fell short of her expectations.

Dalia defended her husband whenever her parents said something negative about him. And it seemed as if they always had something to say, either about his outings on weekends, or his lack of public displays of affection towards his wife.

She would make up excuses for him, telling her parents that he had been assigned to a secret project on weekends and stress consumed him, and that he was a shy man who did not care to broadcast his feelings for her to the world. Her parents did not seem convinced.

But certain events can heal and make people look the other way. When at last Dalia's water broke and her labor pains began, everything seemed suddenly forgotten. Her parents immediately called Alexis at work. As soon he received the message, he spoke to one of the government officials for whom he worked, and the official's secretary arranged for a government Russian car to rush him to the hospital.

Alexis stood by Dalia's side for hours, occasionally going outside her room to tell her parents and his, who arrived shortly after he did, about her progress. She had been admitted to the hospital at 11 a.m. The baby was finally born around midnight. Shortly after the doctor cut the umbilical cord and the baby began to cry, Alexis heard the female doctor announce, "It's a boy! Congratulations, Mom and Dad!"

Alexis had never felt such joy and pride before. It was a feeling beyond his comprehension. To think that this tiny creature had emerged from the union of Dalia and him overwhelmed him. He caressed his wife's arm and she smiled at him as if all the tears she had shed during the times he arrived late at night had been erased by this singular event. She looked exhausted when the nurse placed the baby boy in her arms but her expression glowed with happiness.

Alexis's eyes filled with tears when he examined the tiny baby, partially wrapped in a blanket in his mother's arms: his green eyes, the pinkish face, the tiny hands and fingers. He had a son. He was a father. The fact that Dalia had made this possible led him to appreciate her more than ever before. He was happy she was the mother of his son.

"How are you going to name him?" asked one of the nurses.

"Alexis," said his wife without hesitation looking at him with immense pride.

Alexis did not want his son to bear his name but he felt his wife had endured enough pain not to give her that joy.

"Do you want to hold him?" Dalia asked.

"I'm afraid to touch him," he said as his green eyes opened wide.

The sweetness in his voice made her cry of happiness. The nurses around them could not help themselves and had to wipe their tears.

"Don't be afraid, you silly man," she said. "Here is your son."

She extended her arms and handed the baby to her husband and a nurse taught him how to hold him. When he felt the warmth of his little body against his, he trembled with joy.

"He is precious. Thank you," he said.

Their eyes met, and they said so much without saying a word.

Moments later, he turned to his son, touched his tiny hands, and caressed his face, enthralled by every perfect part of his body. Until that very moment, unlike his wife, he had never believed in the existence of God.

After looking at what he could only categorize as a miracle, he wondered if he had been wrong all along.

* * *

Three months after the birth of his son, Alexis had not been able to build the courage to talk to his wife. He felt that the well-being of his child came first. He had started to go out again but not as frequently as before. As time passed, Dalia had come to the realization that nothing she could do or give her husband would gain his heart.

One Saturday evening, while her son and the rest of her family slept, she went out to the porch close to the time he typically returned from his outings, sat on a rocking chair in her pajamas, and waited for her husband. The moon was out and there was not one cloud in the sky. Everything seemed so eerily quiet. Suddenly, she heard steps. She thought that it had to be him but stayed where she was.

He jumped involuntarily when he first saw her. It was almost 2 a.m.

"I didn't mean to scare you," she whispered. "We need to talk."

He did not know what to do, but for some reason, he felt a knot in his stomach. He had delayed *that* conversation because of his son, to witness the joy of seeing him grow for a little longer, realizing that one day things would change. Now, he wondered if he was ready.

Both of them stayed quiet for a moment. She detected the smell of sweat and liquor that emanated from him and shook her head, without realizing that drinking some fruit punch and rum on the few weekends he went out allowed him to detach himself for a couple of hours from his reality.

"What do you want to talk about?" he asked for the sake of saying something, and the moment those words came out of his mouth, he realized it would have been better if he had not said anything.

She stood and signaled him to walk across the porch, away from the opened window. It was too hot inside the house to keep the windows closed in the evenings, and not even the table-top fans in each bedroom relieved the unbearable heat on warm summer nights.

He followed her, and when they were both by the railing, she was the first to speak.

"I can no longer live like this, making believe nothing is happening around me," she said in a low tone of voice. "It's not fair to you or me."

He stayed quiet. In his mind, this moment had been played over and over again but not like this.

"Who is she? I think I have earned the right to know," she asked, not angry but with sadness.

He took a deep breath.

"Dalia, I owe you an explanation," he whispered.

She shook her head.

"Please no more," she said. "I do not need an explanation because in situations like these, there is often no explanation. Who is she?"

He swallowed dry and moved his head closer to her ear.

"I never wanted to marry you because I knew how much learning the truth would hurt you," he said in a low tone of voice. "You insisted you did not want to be an unwed mother by the time our son was born."

She inhaled deeply and exhaled.

"I know," she said. "I understand, but the time to tell me everything has arrived."

He pressed his lips together wondering what would happen next. She was right. It was time. The palm of his hands turned sweaty as he continued.

"You have been an amazing wife. I do not deserve you or any of the wonderful things you had given me, but the reality is . . . "

He stopped, feeling that the sky was about to fall on him. He needed to say it, at last.

"I'm a homosexual."

It took a moment for her to register what he had said. She repeated it to herself. No, it could not be! She shrank her eyebrows closer together. She must have misunderstood.

She shook her head and looked at him confused.

"You ... what?" she said raising her voice.

He signaled her to stay quiet.

"You heard me," he whispered in her ear. "I am in love with another man. Nothing you can ever do will change how I feel. I'm so sorry."

She covered her face with her hands and moved her head from side to side in disbelief.

"But . . . how could you? How could you . . .?"

She balled her hands into fists and pounded him on the chest while she wept. He let her. He understood her anger.

"Oh my God!" she said with a distraught expression. "I must have sounded so stupid to you all this time. I made such a fool of myself," she yelled clasping her fingers together on top of her head.

"If I could disappear from the face of the earth right now, I would," he said. "You don't know what it is like to live with this inside. It's like a knife stabbing my heart every single day."

Dalia raised her head and looked up at the tall ceilings and then at him.

"Get out," she said in a stern tone of voice, with her eyes full of tears. "Get out! I can't talk to you right. I don't want to see you or know anything about you. Get out!"

"Please don't take my son away from me," he said, taking her hand and placing it between his.

"Just go! Just don't make this more difficult than it needs to be," she said pointing her index finger toward the porch's black iron gate.

By this time, someone inside the house had turned on the lights. He went downstairs onto the sidewalk and disappeared in the darkness of Zapote Street.

Dalia turned around and began to weep inconsolably. In that state, she went back inside her house, almost running into her father who was about to open the front door after having heard his daughter yelling.

He was wearing a pair of shorts and an unbuttoned white shirt. His grey hair was in disarray.

"Why are you crying?" he asked. "What happened?"

She embraced him and wept.

"But, *mi amor*, why did you fight?" he asked.

"I kicked him out, dad," she said, her voice cracking.

"But why?"

"He was cheating on me," she said.

He patted her on the back.

"Come on, come on. Here, let's sit down," he said leading her to the sofa.

By then, her mother had joined them in the living room, and each parent sat on either side and caressed her head and back while she continued to weep.

Her father waited until she calmed down.

"Sometimes, men do these things," he said. "Women out there are something else."

She shook her head.

"You don't understand," she said.

"All I know is that fights are normal in every marriage," said her father. "Both of you need to talk, for your child."

She started to cry again.

"You don't understand, dad," she said, shaking her head. "There is no fixing this, not ever."

"You need to forgive him," said her mother. "I taught you to be a Christian woman. Forgive him. I'm sure it won't happen again."

"Neither one of you understands anything!" Dalia yelled.

"What is there to understand?"

Dalia, with a distraught expression, raised her arms and interlaced her fingers over her head.

"What have I done?" she asked. "Why did you insist I get married? Oh my God!"

"Dalia, please, explain yourself," her mother asked, touching her chest.

She massaged her forehead with her fingers and looked at her parents, as if all the energy had been suddenly removed from her body.

"Alexis . . . is a homosexual," she said, and turning her head towards her father, she added, "There is **no** fixing that."

Her father stood up immediately and gave her an incredulous look.

"What did you say?" he asked, waving his arms up in the air in an exaggerated fashion, his nostrils flaring.

"Oh my God!" her mother said. "I think I'm going to have a heart attack!"

"That motherfucker!" said her father. "Oh no! He's going to have to deal with me! No one, absolutely no one does this to my daughter!"

"It wasn't him, Dad!" Dalia shouted, as tears rolled down her moist and reddened cheeks. "I chased him. I fell in love with him from the moment I saw him. I should have never placed my eyes on him."

"Why didn't he tell you before he married you?" he yelled, his fists closing, his face getter redder.

Broken

Dalia stayed silent for a moment and wiped her face. Suddenly, she heard her baby cry, and simultaneously, she heard footsteps coming from her grandparents' bedroom. She took a deep breath.

"I have to feed the baby, dad," she said with a sad voice. "We have awakened everyone in the house with all the yelling, and frankly, I'm very tired. But you need to understand this. It *was* my fault. You need to believe that. And please, don't let this be known outside this house. I have enough problems."

He father stood in front of her, speechless. She extended her arms and hugged him.

"Thank you for being here for me, dad," she said. "I love you."

Then, turning to her mother who was now standing, her hand on her husband's shoulder, Dalia added. "I love you, mom."

* * *

As he walked towards his parents' house, Alexis felt as if his world had crumbled. His legs felt heavy when he climbed the four steps to the front porch. Moments after he placed the key in the keyhole and opened the door, he heard the flushing toilet.

"Mom," he whispered, thinking it was his mother, as she suffered from insomnia. When the door of the bathroom opened, he heard a male voice.

"Alexis, is that you?"

Alexis swallowed dry.

"Yes, dad. It's me," he whispered.

Towards the back of the house, the light in the bathroom was still on, and he could see his father standing in front of the door wearing a white undershirt and white shorts. Father and son walked from opposite directions of the house towards each other and met in the dining room.

"What are you doing here?" his father asked. "Is the baby fine?"

"Yes, dad. He is," Alexis said.

"Did you and Dalia fight?"

"Yes, we did," said Alexis, pausing for a moment before adding, "It's over between us."

"Wait a minute," his father said. "What do you mean it's over between you?"

At that moment, towards the back of the house, Alexis noticed that the bedroom door of his parents' room had opened and his mother walked out wearing a pink house dress with little red flowers.

"Fernando," Lily said, "who are you talking to?"

Before Fernando had a chance to respond, Lily added, "Alexis, what are you doing here? Is the baby ok?"

"Yes, mom," he said.

"So, why are you here?"

"He was about to tell me," Fernando said. "Let's sit in the living room."

Fernando turned on the lights, and he and Lily sat on the blue sofa, while Alexis sat on a wooden chair across from them.

"You were saying that it is over between you?" his father said. "How can that be? You have a son! Did you fight?"

"It's not that, dad," Alexis said.

"What do you mean, it's over?" Lily asked.

"Did she cheat on you?" Fernando asked.

Alexis shook his head.

"Did *you* cheat on her?" his mother asked with her eyes opened wide.

Alexis remained silent for a moment and looked down at the tiled floor.

"Oh my God!" his mother said placing her hand on her mouth. "A brand new baby, and you cheated on your wife?"

"You don't understand, mom," Alexis said.

"Who is she?" asked Lily.

Alexis took a deep breath and shook his head.

"Well, Lily," said his father. "Sometimes, these things happen. Just break it off, son. The two of you have a son together. You need to work it out."

"But who is she? Do we know her?" her mother asked.

A moment of silence followed, and Alexis rose from his seat. The moment he had dreaded all his life had arrived. He had prepared himself over the years to have that conversation, realizing he would never be ready. His mask had to be removed, as if he had a large band-aid on his face, fast. It would hurt. God knows how much, but he had no choice. Not anymore.

"Mom, dad. It is not a woman," he said. "I'm a homosexual."

His father rose from the couch and faced his son.

"What did you just say?" he asked.

"Oh my God!" said Lily.

Fernando pushed Alexis by his shoulders.

"Did you just say you liked men?" his father asked raising his voice. "My son, flesh of my flesh, likes men?"

"Yes, dad," Alexis said looking at him with a serious expression.

His father closed his fists.

"How dare you!" Fernando yelled pronouncing each word at a time and clenching his jaw. Alexis saw the hatred in his eyes. "How dare you, coming into *my* house to tell me that the boy I raised has turned into a homosexual?"

Then looking at his wife, Fernando added, "Did you know this?"

Lily shook her head, while she wept inconsolably. His father took a step towards him, his nostrils flaring.

"What are you going to do? Please stop!" Lily yelled.

"I'm going to teach him what it is like to be a man!" his father said.

Being a trained fighter, Alexis waited for his father to throw the first punch, and when he did, he grabbed his hand.

"Stop it, please!" his mother yelled. "You are father and son. You can't treat each other like this."

"Let me go, you *maricón*!" his father yelled, trying to free himself.

Alexis freed him and took two steps back. It hurt him to hear that demeaning word for homosexual from his own father.

"I don't want to hurt you, dad," Alexis said. "But you need to listen to me."

"Listen to what?" yelled his father. "What are you going to tell me next?"

Alexis stared at his father with anger.

"You have no idea what it's like to keep it all inside, to live a lie every day of my fucking life!" Alexis said, pounding his own chest with his fist. "I can't do it anymore! You hear? Not for you, not for anyone!"

"Get out of my house!" his father screamed and charged towards his son again, but his wife scurried around him and stood in the middle.

"Don't do this, please," she begged her husband. "He's our son."

"No!" Fernando screamed shaking his head repeatedly. "My son died tonight. Alexis, get out of my house now, before you regret you were ever born."

Alexis's eyes filled with tears, but he held them back. He refused to cry in front of his father.

"I already do, dad. I already do," he said and stormed out of the house, slamming the door behind him.

"Please don't go," begged his mother rushing towards the door.

"Let him go," her husband commanded.

Alexis's mother flung herself on the sofa and wept hopelessly.

Broken

* * *

A week after Alexis's father expelled him from his house, government officials entered one of the homes where ten-peso gay parties were held and jailed him and his boyfriend, along with many of their friends. The government released them shortly after, but their record had been tarnished. The following week, when Alexis discussed the situation with his boss, he suggested it would be best if he quit his job.

On the night his father expelled him from his house, his mother had convinced her sister to give him shelter. She reluctantly allowed him to share her small apartment with her, but told him she did not want to see his boyfriend there.

"This is a serious place," she said.

He knew he could not make her understand, but thanked her for her generosity. To make a living, with money his mother gave him, he began to buy ingredients in the illegal market to make mango marmalade that he sold for two pesos a jar. He worked day and night cooking, and paid his aunt some of the proceeds to help her with expenses.

By 1980, Alexis could hardly find the mangoes he needed to make marmalade. Carlos, his boyfriend, a twenty-year old young man with a nice smile and a kind heart, helped him as much as he could, but Carlos too struggled to survive, sometimes selling his paintings to tourists for a little money via clandestine means, or resorting to selling himself to the tourists, something Alexis could not get himself to do.

Alexis pressured him to stop, but unlike Alexis who could easily conceal his true self, Carlos's mild-mannered demeanor, the inner happiness pouring from him like a waterfall, made it difficult to hide who he was.

Since the moment Carlos had realized he was a homosexual a few years earlier, he stopped caring about what people said or thought, but in doing so, he lost the opportunity to obtain a good job. The government-run businesses, managed by people integrated within the socialist system, did not welcome homosexuals during those years. Carlos had few choices.

On April 1, 1980, an event occurred that would change the lives of many Cubans, including those of Alexis and Carlos. Tired of the weak economy, the housing and job shortages, and the scarcity of basic goods, a group of desperate men drove a bus through the gates of the Peruvian Embassy in Havana. When one of the guards at the embassy was killed, Castro demanded that the embassy turn over the men to the government. Embassy officials refused. In response, on April 4, 1980, Castro removed his guards. The word spread through Havana quickly. Alexis knew this was his chance, but he needed to see Dalia and his son first.

He arranged a secret meeting at his aunt's house. He sent Dalia a note through one of her friends, explaining that it was a matter of life and death. He begged her to bring his son.

Alexis had explained to his aunt what he was about to do, and she decided it was best if she stayed out of the apartment while Alexis spoke to his ex-wife.

She arrived at the agreed-upon time, with her son in a blue stroller. When Alexis opened the door and saw his son for the first time in over seven months, his eyes filled with tears. The boy had green eyes like him and brown hair like his mother. He was beautiful.

He asked Dalia in, closed the door behind her, and his eyes turned to his son.

"Can I hold him?" he asked.

She took a deep breath, looked at him nervously, and nodded. He picked up his son in his arms and embraced him. The boy smelled like *Agua de Violeta* cologne and was dressed in a blue, embroidered outfit he recognized. It had been Carlos's compensation from one of the tourists. Carlos knew how much this gift for his son would mean to Alexis, and although Alexis could not deliver it himself, he had his aunt do it for him. Alexis embraced the toddler for a moment and held him in his arms.

"Look at you! You're so big."

Dalia smiled.

"This is your dad, Alex," she said unsure of whether the toddler understood.

Alexis smiled at his son.

"Alex? Is that what you call him?" he said.

"Yes. I like the shorter version of the name," she said.

He smiled and nodded, realizing the real reasons why Dalia no longer cared to call his son Alexis.

"So, how are you?" she asked.

He shrugged.

"It doesn't matter how I am," he said. "The important thing is that you allowed me to see my son one last time."

Dalia tucked her hair behind her ears and shrunk her eyebrows closer together.

"What do you mean?" she asked.

"Sit down," he said. "We need to talk."

She sat on the sofa of the cozy living room, and he returned his son to the stroller.

"Are you going somewhere?" she asked.

He remained silent and watched his son play with a plastic colorful toy.

"Thank you for letting me say good-bye to him," he said.

"I don't understand."

Alexis took a deep breath.

"As you may know by now, I'm sure my mother told you, I was kicked out of my house. I don't have a job. I don't have a life here anymore."

He glanced at his son and smiled sadly.

"I will miss him," he said.

"What's going on? Where are you going?" She asked with a look of concern.

"I'm going into the Peruvian Embassy tonight. This is my only chance. I'm asking for political asylum."

Dalia's eyes filled with tears.

"You're leaving?" she asked.

"Yes. It is better this way. I can't help you or my son while I'm here. I need to start a new life. The only two people keeping me here are my mother and my son. My mother understands that I need to do this. I already said good-bye to her and to my sister. My dad won't talk to me."

"I'm so sorry," she said.

"Don't be."

"I loved you. You know that," she said.

"I know you did. I'm sorry, I could not offer you the same. But I promise one thing. I will take care of you and my son, even if I have to work day and night when I get to the United States. I am tired of feeling like a broken man. In the United States, people like me don't have to hide from themselves. This is my chance to be whole."

Dalia stood up, as she tried to contain her tears.

"Can I hug you?" she asked.

He nodded, and she embraced him.

"Please don't let my son forget me," he said, as she held him, his voice cracking with emotion. "Tell him that I will always love him."

After she set him loose, he picked up his son in his arms again and kissed his chubby cheeks.

* * *

By April 6, 1980, over 10,000 men, women, and children had entered the Peruvian Embassy desperate to leave Cuba, among them, Alexis and his boyfriend. The plastic bottle of water and pressure-cooked can of condensed milk they brought with them only lasted a day. During the second day, they went without food.

They sought the shade of the trees and the walls of the embassy to avoid dehydration and drank warm water from a faucet.

Tensions intensified inside: too many refugees and no conditions to receive them. The Cuban government offered passes to asylum-seekers allowing them to go to their homes and return to the embassy. Most of the people inside refused to take advantage of these passes, afraid they would not be allowed back in. Alexis told Carlos he would rather die of starvation than return to a place where he was not welcomed.

A few days after the removal of security from the embassy, police, security guards, and trucks filled with uniformed soldiers began to guard it once again, increasing the nervousness of those inside. The government-controlled newspaper, *Granma*, published an article suggesting that those seeking refuge were "delinquents, antisocial and parasitic elements." It also added that the group included many homosexuals. Alexis read this article after one of those individuals who ventured outside the embassy returned with a newspaper and shared it with him. He cringed.

During the days that followed, a humanitarian crisis developed, as food ran out inside, and the smell of feces and urine reigned over the grounds of the embassy. Various foreign countries offered to take a small percentage of the refugees. The Red Cross sent workers to care for the elderly, pregnant women, and children. Food and water were eventually supplied in a disorganized manner, causing people to fight each other over the meager quantities.

On April 20, 1980, an unprecedented move on the part of the Cuban government would change history. Castro announced that those wanting to leave Cuba could come to the port of Mariel to be picked up in boats. Seventeen-hundred vessels overwhelmed Cuban and U.S. authorities. Castro emptied his jails of "undesirables" and encouraged homosexuals to leave the island. Cuban officials then packed refugees into the boats of those who waited to pick up their relatives, forcing many boaters to leave Cuba without their families and with their vessels full of strangers.

On April 26, 1980, Alexis and his boyfriend boarded a shrimp boat off the coast of Havana heading for the United States. They were unrecognizable, with burnt skin and sunken eyes from lack of sleep and poor nutrition.

Alexis could not believe that the nightmarish days at the embassy had ended. For a brief moment, he looked at Carlos with fear in his eyes, uncertain of the life that awaited him beyond the ocean. Carlos smiled, reassuring him all would be fine. Alexis nodded. He could always count on him to brighten his darkest day.

As Alexis sat on the rusty floor watching the lights of the coast become smaller, he waved good-bye to the broken version of himself he left behind. Ahead, his future stood, tall, accepting, and ready to receive him with open arms.

Zapote(s) Street Photographs

Picture of the home where the author lived in Havana: Zapote 269 (aka Zapotes). Below is Zapote St, where most of the stories take place, with its broken streets and colonial-style homes.

Zapote(s) Street Photographs

Zapote St, near Santos Suárez Park.

People waiting in line on the corner of Zapote & Serrano St (like in Pizza Coupons)

Zapote(s) Street Photographs

Santos Suárez, a couple of blocks from the author's home.

Corner of Flores and Zapote St, near Santos Suárez Park.

References

www.coha.org "From Persecution to Acceptance? The History of LGBT Rights in Cuba."

http://www.huffingtonpost.com/2010/12/30/hotel-nacional-cuba_n_802769.html

http://www.findingdulcinea.com/news/on-this-day/April/On-This-Day--Thousands-Authorized-to-Leave-Cuba-in-Mariel-Boatlift.html

Interviews with family members, including William Portomeñe, owner of Portomene la Suite hair and makeup studio in Coral Gables in Miami, and Maria Fernandez, my aunt, and Berta's character.

"Cousin Andrés" was loosely based on my mother's journals. She continues to fuel my creativity from beyond. I miss you, mom.

Acknowledgements

I would like to thank the following people, without whose assistance, love, and support *Candela's Secrets and Other Havana Stories* would not have been possible:

My mother, who taught me the values of hard work, passion, and dedication. She inspires me, from beyond, to keep writing.

My husband, Ivan, for providing advice on some of the scenes and finding a comfortable place where I could write.

My family: my sister Lissette, my brother Rene, my inlaws, Madeline and Guillermo, my aunt María, for listening to my stories. Tracey Terwilliger ONeil who has been a sister for me through the years and great supporter. William Portomeñe, my cousin and his father Alfredo.

All the friends I have found during the last couple of year and have helped me in my journey: Patricia Ford, Susan Girard, and Jackie Challarca, among many others.

Sarita Portomeñe for visiting my neighborhood and taking such wonderful pictures.

The artist of the cover, Mr. Felix Acosta, a talented Cuban painter, for a beautiful rendition of Candela's character.

Leita Kaldi, Author of *Roller Skating in the Desert* and *In the Valley of Atibon* for editing the short story

Acknowledgements

"Candela's Secrets" and providing me with excellent suggestions.

Mrs. Diana Plattner and Dr. Shannon Tivnan, my very talented editors.

Those individuals who kindly read some of the stories including: Kayrene Kelley Smither, Ed Zebrowski, Stan Wnek, Juan Rivera, and Rafael Mieses.

My Tampa General Hospital family for all the support.

My Tampa General Hospital Foundation and the TGH Auxiliary, two wonderful organizations that support such an important mission.

The readers who read my first novel, those who took the time to write reviews, and those who kept asking me "when will the next book be published?," thank you very much.

About the Author

Betty Viamontes, author of the highly rated autobiographical novel *Waiting on Zapote Street*, was born in Havana, Cuba. Her work is known for its honesty and its ability to keep readers engaged from the moment they start to read.

Betty, her siblings, and her mother migrated to the United States from Cuba in 1980, when Betty was fifteen years old. They left Havana on a shrimp boat on a stormy night, when many men, women, and children lost their lives, traveling on overloaded vessels similar to theirs. Upon her arrival to the United States, Betty had to master the English language and become acclimated to a new culture.

Betty completed graduate studies in Business and Accounting, as well as a Graduate Certificate in Creative Writing, at the University of South Florida, and moved on to a successful career in Accounting. Her creative works have appeared on various literary journals and newspapers.

In 2015, as a tribute to her mother, who passed away in 2011, and to fulfill her last wishes, Betty Viamontes published a memoir-style novel, based on her family's life in Cuba, entitled *Waiting on Zapote Street*. This novel was selected by a United Nations book club for its February 2016 reading and received excellent reviews. It has also been presented at a local university and one of its chapters will appear on the University of South Florida publication *The Mailer Review* (2016).

Betty enjoys giving back to her community. She is a regular speaker at the University of South Florida and other professional organizations, and is active at the Florida Institute of Certified Public Accountants. She derives her passion from her mother who was a teacher for many years and instilled in her the importance of an education, perseverance, and hard work.

Made in the USA
Middletown, DE
04 June 2017